Ride a
Northbound Horse

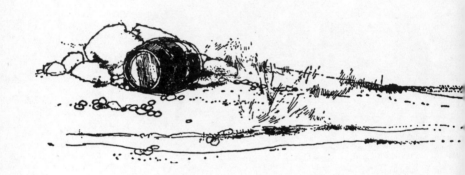

Ride a Northbound Horse

RICHARD WORMSER

Illustrated by
Victor G. Ambrus

London
OXFORD UNIVERSITY PRESS
1964

Oxford University Press, Amen House, London E.C.4

GLASGOW   NEW YORK   TORONTO   MELBOURNE   WELLINGTON
BOMBAY   CALCUTTA   MADRAS   KARACHI   LAHORE   DACCA
CAPE TOWN   SALISBURY   NAIROBI   IBADAN   ACCRA
KUALA LUMPUR   HONG KONG

Printed in Great Britain by Richard Clay and Company, Ltd.,
Bungay, Suffolk

I

FIRST night alone on the trail, he was lucky; when he turned the oxen out to bottom-graze the rank grass, he found a peanut-patch where the people had not picked clean; and so Cav Rand built a little fire, using his father's flint and steel to save the dozen matches in the bottle. As always, the first spark that the spring knocked off the stone didn't catch the cotton wick; but the second did, and he blew the flame alive.

He had a whole hatful of the goobers, enough, really, to feed a man and his friend. But anybody who's ever roasted peanuts in a swampland fire will tell you: some burn, and some are wormy, and some just plain don't have any kernels in them.

Still, it was a meal, and warm in his belly, and he pulled two fallen logs together and filled the space between with cypress tips, and so slept, the grave oxen munch-munching all night near him. Once Bo and Billy strayed too far away, so he couldn't hear their bells, and he woke up at once.

Too many people had gone away from Cav in the last week; he felt he'd just plain fall into pieces if he lost the two cream oxen that were all that had come from Alabama with him.

He got out of the cypress tip bed, his bare feet squelching in the muddy bottom, and circled till he heard the bells. Slipping on Billy's neck, he rode him back to where he thought his bed had been, Bo trotting along behind; seemed like an ox could get lonesome too.

Then he couldn't find the bed again, the moon having gone behind the clouds that seemed so fond of this Louisiana country, and he ended up sleeping not wet, but damp enough to tell him this wasn't any Great American Desert, such as he hoped to find in the West.

Next morning he made a fire and boiled up some more goobers into a sort of a paste and had hardly drunk it when it started to rain, a soft, slow rain that seemed the kind that could keep itself going a long, long time. At least, such a rain would have behaved such a way back home; here, in this strange country, maybe it was just a morning drizzle that would burn off by ten.

It didn't. He sat the wagon, the animals being well-enough trained to go ahead on the voice, without a goadsman to prod them along.

Just as well, Cav thought. He had on a quilt he thought he remembered his mother making, back five, six years ago, when he was a little boy; and over it an old canvas that his father had boiled in some linseed oil to make it turn water; and on top of his head an old torn wool hat, its leather band stuffed with grass to make it fit.

Wrapped up that way, he hoped he bulked big enough to

pass for a man and not for a shirt-tail thirteen-year-old boy. He had nothing to fear from the Butterfield Stages that stormed past regularly twice a day, one eastbound, one west; but the solitary horsemen who singlefooted or loped past in the mud mostly didn't look as though they were above stealing all a boy had, and maybe slitting his throat for a passing regard, so's he couldn't tell who did it.

Cav Rand had lost enough already.

When the sun came out, it said that it was four o'clock, and Bo and Billy seemed to take this to heart; they began to edge off the trail, and drop their heads for mouthfuls of green stuff, which they brought up slobbering between their soft lips in the unmannerly fashion of cattle.

This was higher country than he had been going through, and firmer underfoot. He got down from the wagon, and looked at the graze. Johnson grass, and he remembered his father saying that that was a kind of weed when it grew in cotton, but pure beefsteak on a grass animal's ribs.

He shoved along, walking and using the goad now, hoping to come to a creek bottom where something wild—nuts or fruits or mapleseeds—grew that would fill a human belly.

But the country stayed high, and the rivulet he finally crossed grew between grassy edges.

Well, you could say a good ox-driver would pick this for his cattle, and call yourself smart to camp here.

So he camped. A lone mulberry tree, just in flower, grew up from the creek bank, and he made himself a canvas bed there, and hung the quilt out across the wagon tongue to dry.

His stomach kept making reproachful remarks to him.

When dark came he built a fire, not because he was cold, and surely not because he had anything to cook over it, but because it cut away a little of the awful aloneness that he felt.

That was maybe not the smartest thing he could have done. The country was broken and rolling, and he was a hillock or two away from the trail; but his little blaze must have glowed over the swells of earth, because—call it ten o'clock, by the stars—a man turned off from the trail and rode towards him, the horse's hoofs giving the steady beat that told a good rider was holding the reins.

At once Cav stood up, and thought to run. But then something in him came up, and he stood his ground, even sat down again, pulling the canvas over his shoulders. If he ran, the man could take the wagon and the household goods, and Bo and Billy.

The man and horse pulled up on the other side of the fire. There was not much to be seen of the face, under a big hat and the stars. But the voice was a big voice and deep. 'Mind if I share your fire?'

Cav said: 'There's two sides to it, beside the smoky one.'

A laugh came from high above the saddle and the man swung down, leather creaking in the saddle and the stirrups and on his legs, too, where he wore what Cav's father had said were called 'chaps', out to the West.

He took off the saddle in a few easy movements, untied a water bottle from behind it, rubbed the water well into the horse's back and then stripped off the bridle, silver gleaming in starlight, and slapped the horse on the rump. 'Go buy yourself a meal, pony.' The horse went away, snorting, and then could be heard down at the creek, rolling back and forth.

The man dropped the saddle where the smoke from the fire was least, and sat on it. 'Nine times,' he said, 'old horse rolled nine times. Means I got me a ninety dollar horse.'

4

'I've heard that,' Cav said.

The man grunted. 'Sure hate to hold any bank to it.' His hands were dark in the firelight; then he moved them and Cav saw that he was stripping off black leather gloves, shiny with wear. Cav had never seen a man wear gloves before. They went under the double belts the visitor was wearing. One gunbelt, and one to hold up the chaps, and braces over the shoulders for the pants. It was a sight to scare a boy, all that gun and belt and bullets in the loops, but somehow, Cav wasn't frightened.

Cav had picketed the oxen; the newcomer's pony went down towards them, and there was the sound of snuffling as horse met cattle, and then the chomp-chomp of the pony's teeth went along with the slow twist and pull of the oxen.

The man reached behind the saddle he was sitting on and unhooked his saddle-bags. 'Mind if I use your fire?'

Cav didn't answer; he was too fascinated. The rider's bedroll was on top of the leather Army bags; he rolled it to one side, opened a pouch, took out a slab of bacon, wrapped in a bit of tarp, cut off three thick slices. He started to put the slab away, then hesitated and cut off two more.

Then he stood up, easy, and sliced a branch off the mulberry tree, threaded his bacon on it. Two stones held the green branch over the fire.

The rider said: 'My name's Bruce Cavanagh.' He took a little coffee-pot out of the left hand bag.

The boy said slowly: 'That's funny. Mine's Cav Rand.' He reached out for the pot, said: 'I'll fill that.'

'Thank you kindly,' Cavanagh said automatically. 'Cav for Cavanagh?'

Cav had taken three steps towards the brook. His back to the rider, he said: 'Well, no. Cav for Cavalier. My Maw was notional. Paw used to call it flighty.'

6

He went on to the creek, the deep voice behind him saying: 'I've had a fight or two over that Bruce handle.'

Brook water was cold on his wrists, and for a minute seemed to take his strength away. Holding the coffee-pot steady, he went and rested his head on Bo's neck for a minute, Bo being the kindlier of the two steers. Then he touched the top of the water in the pot. He had never spilled a drop, and he felt better, climbing back up to the fire.

Little blue sparks spat as the bacon grease fell into the dying fire. Cavanagh didn't look up as Cav came back. He had rigged two flat rocks for a pot rest, and he put the pot on, poured coffee into it from a canvas sack.

Then he turned the bacon, said: 'T'won't be long. Take it proud if you'd eat.'

'I'm plumb full.'

Bruce Cavanagh said: 'Take it kindly, none the less,' and turned the green-wood stick again. 'Paw-paw wood?'

'Mulberry.'

Cavanagh grunted as though Cav had passed some sort of test. His saddle-bags seemed bottomless. He took out cold corncake, broke it in two, laid it on a clean rock and began sliding the bacon off the stick with the point of his knife, laying it on the corncake so the fat would soak in.

Cav's throat contracted drily, his stomach knotted up. Last night's goober peas, this morning's mush, seemed a long ways back.

'More here than I can eat,' Cavanagh said. 'And I'm hitting Alexandria by noon tomorrow. Whereafter, I don't plan on eating horse-smelling bacon.' He handed over one of the corncakes, covered with the thick meat.

Cav Rand very carefully didn't bite into his supper till the man had.

The coffee boiled. Bruce Cavanagh gave the pot a quick swirl, sending grounds out into the fire. 'Should settle it with some cold, but it's too late and too tired for any foo-faraw. We'll have to share the cup, turn and turn about.'

The tin cup had come out of the saddle-bags, too.

'I've got china mugs in the wagon box.'

The rider chuckled. 'Now there's something I like. Seems like your fingers never get hard enough to hold a hot tin cup in perfect ease and comfort.'

Cav remembered his manners, and laid his corncake and bacon on a rock before he went to the wagon box. He brought the thick mugs back, handed them over.

'Handy,' Cavanagh said, and filled them.

The warmth on top of the food loosened the knots in Cav's stomach. He put the mugs to one side, said: 'I'll wash them in daylight.'

Bruce Cavanagh untied the thongs from his bedroll, flipped it out, feet to the dying fire, said: 'Time enough.'

Country he had been travelling through had been so wet that Cav had been sleeping in the hard wagon bed. Now he went over and dragged his own bedding out, laid it along-side the rider's, stretched out. It wasn't cold enough yet to need getting under the covers. After a minute he remem-bered and took his shoes off. His fingers felt the way they did when he stayed swimming too long. . . . That was a while back, swimming and diving and. . . .

His eyes jerked open as Bruce Cavanagh said: 'How old are you, Cav?'

'Thir—seventeen.' He was wide awake again.

Bruce Cavanagh said: 'How old?'

Cav let the silence build up in the night, under the slowly moving leaves of the mulberry tree. There was a star that came and went as the branches moved, but down here on

8

the ground he couldn't feel any breeze at all. 'Thirteen and a half,' he said.

The man said: 'Yeah. . . . Yeah.' Then his voice came out in a long sigh, as though he had made a decision. 'Then tell me about it.'

Cav knew it all, certainly. But it takes a while to sort it out in your mind, so you'll tell it like a man and not like a kid. He said: 'We farmed on the Black Warrior, back in Alabam'. Lost the farm. I dunno. Dad had a claim and this big plantation had a claim, and the law said theirs was the right one. . . . So we started for Texas.'

'With a good wagon, and two good ox, and not much more.'

'Yeah. . . . Yes, that's right, Mr. Cavanagh.'

'Could maybe find you a market for same, in Alexandria. . . . Who was all this "we"?'

'Maw, Paw, my sister, kid brother.'

'Now, just tell it,' Bruce Cavanagh said. 'Just tell it how it happened.'

'Swamp fever,' Cav said.

'Louisiana bottomland fever,' Bruce Cavanagh said. 'All of 'em, boy?'

'All of them, Mr. Cavanagh.'

Bruce Cavanagh said: 'Yeah,' and made that long sigh again. 'Don't bother with that Mr. Cavanagh. Folks mostly call me Cav, Bruce being a little fancy for my place in life.'

'You're a farmer?'

Bruce Cavanagh's laugh was the finest thing Cav had heard in days. The man laughed so hard he had to lean forward against his knees. Then he sank back again. 'No, Cav, I am no ploughman. And where you're going, across the Sabine, it doesn't always do to ask that. . . .'

Cav had to smile because he had enjoyed the laughing

9

so. But he asked: 'I don't understand. My father was a farmer.'

The big man nodded. 'Sure. Mine, too, for that matter. But that is in the South. West, it simply isn't farmland, and any man who tries to make it so will drought out in a few years; see his furrows blow away, his seed dry up in the earth. Then he'll move on and leave his land blowing and no good to anyone.'

'I see.'

'And leave his barbed wire fences for cattle to drift up against. When it snows, cows can freeze from being held back by a fence.'

Drowsy, fed, Cav was silent for a while. Then he said: 'I can't call you Cav.'

The man's voice was sleepy, too. 'That's right. Were we to trail together, folks'd call us Little Cav and Big Cav, I reckon.'

Cav said: 'I wouldn't mind that.'

But he got no answer, and for a while he thought Big Cav had fallen off to sleep. Then the man said: 'Look me up in Alexandria. . . . Alex, we call her. The Goin' West Livery Stable'll know where I am. I'll see you get a good price for your outfit. Could use a wagon and steers, where I'm heading.'

Cav said: 'Where's that?' But there was no answer at all, and when he was sure there wasn't going to be, he asked it again, a little different: 'Where's that, Big Cav, that you're going?'

But the rider was asleep.

2

MORNING showed Big Cav's hair to be dark yellow, almost blond, but not quite, like last year's hay still in the bale. They ate more bacon and drank coffee, but Big Cav said he was out of corncake.

Cav said: 'Had I some meal, I could make pones.'

'You cook?'

The boy laughed. 'Sometimes just fine, sometimes I burn everything, sometimes it comes out sort of so-so.'

'That's the way of every cook I've ever hired or eaten after.'

Cav laughed and said: 'Reckon,' and then Big Cav laughed, too, and said: 'You'll make a Texan yet.' He stood up, whistled his pony. The horse went down on his knees, rolled once, and then stood up and trotted up to stand quietly by his saddle.

Cav said: 'He's well trained.'

'Well, he's no dude trick-horse, but he minds all right. Just a travelling horse; he's too big for cutting.'

Big Cav had cleaned his pony's back now, and swung the blanket and saddle up. He cinched down, leaving the back strap loose and slid the bridle up, the horse's mouth obediently opening for the bit. He swung aboard, taking his gloves from his belt and pulling them on, while the reins hung slackly twisted around the saddle-horn.

'Reckon you know to span-up your oxen and put them on the trail, Cav,' he said. 'You'll be in Alex before sundown. . . . Better take what's left of the bacon, for your lunching.'

'No need.'

'It's do that or throw it to the birdies. Come noon-time I'll be chewing food that never saw a saddle-bag, and glad of it. The bacon's under the tree.'

'Thanks, then.' He didn't dare call the big man by name.

'And see me, if you want to sell the outfit, Goin' West Livery Stable. It's too much gear for a one-man camp.'

He had not said 'one-boy'.

Cav nodded, and went to roll his bedding. The china mugs were washed and back in the wagon box. Big Cav rode away, the boy listening to the pony's hoofs drumming lightly in a slow walkout.

Then the hoofbeats got louder again, and Big Cav was looming over him as he backed Bo to the wagon. 'I'm a curious kind of man,' Big Cav said. 'I'll lose my nose over it sometime.'

'Yes,' Cav said.

'Why did you keep going west when—when you found yourself alone? Why not back home?'

Cav thought a minute. He'd never asked himself the question before.

A meadowlark decided his day had started, and jumped up out of the damp ground down by the rivulet, singing as he went. The air, which had been a light blue, turned clear as the sun came over the edge of Louisiana to start full day and end dawn.

Cav said: 'Home was gone, like I told you. And then, Paw started to make Texans out of us Rands. I guess maybe I thought it proper that one of us make it all the way.'

'I reckon,' Big Cav said, as though he had proved something to himself. He suddenly grinned. His teeth were short and white and very even; maybe he had smiled before, but

Cav hadn't seen it in the night. 'That's what I reckoned, Cav,' the man said. 'You sure you aren't kin to the Cavanaghs?'

Cav Rand said: 'Maw used to say, everybody in the South is kin to everyone else.'

Big Cav laughed, and this time, when he turned away, he kept on going. Spanning in, yoking, starting out, Cav couldn't see him, but when Bo and Billy settled into their stride, and he could climb to the wagon seat, he sighted the big hat ahead.

Big Cav was still walking his pony—no, his travelling horse—the way Paw had always said: 'Walk first hour of the morning and last hour of the night, and your horse will last to get you there.'

It was a quiet day, and for once the sunlight held good; but after the last few weeks, the canvas on the wagon was wet enough so it didn't stop steaming till noon, and then began crackling and snapping in every breeze, loose on the bows. Canvas was like rawhide backwards, Cav thought, always too tight or too loose.

He rode along, sometimes passing a horseman, sometimes a buggy with a salesman or maybe a doctor in it.

Then he saw something ahead of him. Something or someone; at the distance it was hard to tell.

Black and bent over, like a beetle, it walked a little wavery like a beetle, too. Cav clucked to the oxen to hurry, but oxen don't hurry much, and they weren't curious, like he was. They just walked along, and the thing grew slowly, and then it had men's legs.

Almost any man can outwalk an oxcart, but not with a pack like this one was carrying.

The face that was turned to him was long and thin, and ended in long, thin whiskers, somewhat brown-stained.

Small blue eyes were as bright as ice crystals. Before Cav could say anything, the big pack was dumped on the floor of the driving seat, and the man had his foot on the hub, climbing in.

Cav hadn't intended to offer a ride, but there didn't seem to be much choice in the matter. The man was perching himself on the pack, riding backwards. Hunched over, he now looked more like a cricket than he did like a beetle.

He spat over the side and said: 'Name's Shawnee.'

'Indian?'

Bony fingers clawed at the whiskers. 'Indians don't wear these. Not any I ever saw. Naw, Shawnee the Peddler. Got the name because I used to trade with the folks of that tribe. . . . Going far?'

If he told this man about Texas, Shawnee might want to ride that far. Cav said: 'I'm going to Alexandria.'

Shawnee spat sideways into the dust. 'Well, every little bit helps, like they say. I reckon you can drop me off where the houses start, and I'll peddle my way in. Ordinarily, it don't pay to show your wares too close to town, bein's how the ladies along there know store prices, but I'm figgering to raise all the cash I can. Figgerin' to buy me a hoss an'

buggy in Alex, and quit this old foot-slogging life. . . .
Where's yore paw, son, or are you bound out?'

This was open country, and a well-travelled road. But
nobody had passed for maybe a half an hour. Cav said:
'Paw's asleep back there,' which could be taken to mean in
the wagon bed. Cav's throat clamped a little when he said
it, and not from the near-lie.

'Wish't I had a boy, to drive whilst I slept,' Shawnee said.
'But who'd take old Shawnee for a husband and father?'

Maybe somebody would if you bathed, Cav thought.

The peddler was a talker. While Alexandria came on the
trail as a line of trees showing the Red River, he rattled on:
'Second thought, it wouldn't be so good. A peddler's got to
be awake, looking out for houses, sizing 'em up. You
know a peddler's best day, boy? Monday. Ladies, now, they
like to be took away from the washtub. And besides, give a
good peddler like old Shawnee a sight of the family wash,
and he can size up to a split nickel what the family purse is.
Keep it in mind, do you take to peddling for a living.'

Now red brick and white shingles could be seen through
the spring-leafed trees. Houses. Maybe this old goat would
hop off at them, and Cav could go on in his own way, with
his own thoughts. 'Don't aim to follow the peddling line.'

'Well, you're right there.' The trail was widening out into
a sure enough road, with stake and rider fencing to keep
stock where they belonged. Shawnee said: 'You make
mighty little and you work mighty hard, peddling on the
road. You would not be in need of any simple thing, would
you? I'd give you a good price, seeing you've been so
kind.'

Show this man money, and you'd never lose him till he
had it. 'We got everything we need.'

A house came over the rolling country, white painted,

behind a green big paddock. Shawnee said: 'Well, I'll give this a try,' and hopped down. He walked alongside, waved his hand and reached in for the pack. He was stronger than he looked, looping his arms through the straps.

Cav said: 'So long.'

'Mebbe we'll meet again,' Shawnee said. 'I sure hate to waste time on a person and make no sale.'

Then he had turned up the driveway to the house, and Cav could go back to watching the land roll by.

Pretty country. Seemed a little like Virginia, where Maw had come from, before she'd travelled south to visit kin, and met Paw. Coming in off the swamps of eastern Louisiana and the scrawny hill country he'd camped in last night with Big Cav, it seemed doubly pretty.

Now the paddocks were giving away to big cotton-fields, green because it was spring, but they would be podding out grey pretty soon and then white. Be nice to see. But he had to get to Texas.

He slipped off the wagon and walked alongside Bo, carrying the prod lightly. Big Cav had said he should sell the outfit, oxen and wagon both, in Alexandria—Alex.

Guess that's right. Man travelling alone had no use for the big bedstead, the iron stove, the food chest, and the little rocker, no use for slow-moving cattle or a cattle-drawn heavy wagon.

All he needed was a horse and a bedroll, and saddle-bags with some bacon and coffee and corncake. Or tea. Maw had been a tea drinker. When she was dying, back there in the bottoms, he had made tea for her, and when it had run out, it had plain ached his heart how she missed it. Tea was easier to carry than coffee.

Still, he would miss Bo and Billy and the big, lumbering, creaking wagon. When they were gone, thirteen years

16

would be wiped out, there'd be nothing left to link him to all he'd been and done; a kid hunting crawdads in the Black Warrior cliffs, a boy going to a one-room school and learning to read and write and fight in the school yard, a baby in a split-shake house, though he didn't remember the baby part too well.

More and more people were on the road as he came into Alex, but they hardly looked at him. This close to a town a boy travelling alone was not much of a strangeness, and for all anybody knew his Paw—or his bond-master—could be lying down under the stretched canvas, leaving him to drive.

Now two streets could be seen, running along a block back from the road, plain at each crossing. Kids his age and younger played in picket-fence yards, under chinaberry and magnolia trees, in and out of Cape Jessamine bushes. Sometimes they called to him in their soft, Louisiana voices, like blackstrap dripping out of a jug, but he paid them no heed; he was going to Texas, he would be in that country when they were still chasing tag and teasing puppies, safe in their own home grounds. They were nothing to him.

There was a hotel, two storey and long, and then a livery stable, but it was called The Deep Straw, and a wagon yard, and he thought he would have to ask one of these soft-tongues for his bearings, but finally he saw The Goin' West, and stopped Bo and Billy at the watering trough.

They dropped their noses and blew, and then put their tongues out and licked the dust away from their split nostrils, and finally drank. Cav left them and went into the office.

The man in the high-backed chair was fat and red-faced and blue-eyed. 'That your ox-cart outside, son?' When Cav nodded, he said: 'We don't get much call to bed down cattle. Try the wagon yard back up the street.' The spit he sent at the brass gaboon was brown-stained.

'Bruce Cavanagh said to meet him here.'

Scuff-shoed feet slid off the desk and clattered on the floor. The liveryman gave a grin that made Cav think that he must like Big Cav as much as Cav did. It would be nice to be a big man that everyone liked so much they were glad to do favours for him.

'Cav? Why didn't you say so? Told me to peel an eye for you.'

The fat man stood up and shoved his shirt down under his belt. 'Just drive back all the way, and yoke out. I'll throw some straw down for your steers to take a nap.'

The ox-shoes click, clicked as they went through the wooden-floored alleyway of the barn. One of Billy's sounded thin and a little loose. There was some money, but not much, left in the hollow board that cornered the food-box on the wagon. Just about pay for one set of shoes, not two. Time to sell, as Big Cav had said. Surely two oxen and a wagon and some furniture was worth a lot more than a travelling—not cutting—horse and saddle and some food.

The fat man was clumsy unhooking the yoke, and Cav said: 'I'll manage.' The oxen walked around the yard a little, saw the straw, and lay down, hind-end first, cow-fashion.

Walking away, Cav put the bars up that led from the backyard to the alleyway. The fat man said: 'No need. I'll be right in the office, and my hostlers are working down the stalls. If those cattle get a urge to go sightseeing, we'll just say shoo to them.'

'When Bo and Billy decide to travel, they keep going,' Cav said, and finished dropping the bars into their slots.

The fat man stared, and said: 'What's your name, son?'

Cav said: 'I am not your son, but my name is Cav Rand.'

The fat man took a step back, and said: 'Kinfolk, huh? Well, tell Cav we treated you right, here. I'll have water drug to yore oxen in a bucket.'

'Sure,' Cav said. 'When'll—Cav be back?' It felt funny to call someone else by his own name, but Bruce Cavanagh hadn't given him permission to call him Big Cav, and wasn't likely to, since such a name would tie them together. But he could go on saying Big Cav in his mind.

'I didn't ask him,' the livery man said, drily. 'But he's over to the hotel.'

The way he said it made it pretty certain there was only one hotel in town, and Cav had seen that, so didn't have to ask for directions. He walked on the board side-walk, drumming his heels a little at the strange feel of solid wood under him; he'd been a long time on mud and sod and gritty sand.

His folks had taught him manners. He took off his hat in the hotel, and told the sleek-haired man at the desk he'd like to see Mr. Bruce Cavanagh.

The man started to laugh, then decided against it, and hit a little metal dome, maybe silver, so that it gave out a sound like a bell. A boy not much more than four or five years older than Cav trotted up, and the man spoke to him, and then said: 'You can sit on that bench over there and wait,' to Cav.

It wasn't a long wait, and could have been longer for all of Cav; there was something going on every minute in that hotel place. Two men passed within a foot of him without seeing him, they were so busy talking a language that Cav guessed was French, since this was Louisiana. Then there was a lady, who smelled like she'd been sleeping in a bank of violet flowers every night since she was born, and a small man with a curling moustache who smoked a cigar like he hated it, keeping it away from him with a gold and diamond cigar holder, which he carried in a hand that had gold and diamond rings on every single finger, except the thumb.

Then two fellows who could only be Texans, with their pants shoved into tall, soft boots whose pull-on straps hung way down, like mules' ears when the mule is tired and low in his mind, came swinging by, in long, loping strides that seemed about to throw them off their undercut high heels, but didn't. One of them said: 'I'm buying my wagon and cooking gear here, but I'll wait to pick up horses over in San Antone.'

The other one said: 'Won't do us any harm to look in on the sale. Louisiana horses have some good blood in them.'

'Every time you go to a horse auction, Bub, you end up animal-poor.'

They both laughed, and went on out, and then Big Cav was coming down the steps towards him. He said: 'So you made it, Cav.'

'Yes, sir. Nooned on the bacon you left me, and came in slick as a whistle.'

Big Cav said: 'Come on upstairs. Meet my partner.'

Cav had never been upstairs in any place before. The county courthouse, back home, had been two-storey, but he'd never been in the courthouse at all. Stairs indoors were a new thing to him, but no harder to climb than stairs out-doors or the hub of a wagon.

Big Cav's partner was Mr. Kane. He wasn't as big as Big Cav, but he would do for big; and he was very soft-spoken, even lazy sounding, though more like the Texas horseman than the Lousiana sugar-speakers. He said: 'Cav told me about you. Understand you have some prime cattle to sell.'

'Two oxen, broke to yoke, pull a wagon or a plough, or a harrow,' Cav said.

From someplace inside Mr. Kane a laugh started and came out, slow and easy like the rest of him. 'You'll make an auctioneer when you're full grown,' he said. 'We'll go look at them, but don't mention ploughing. We go to a different church; we're cattle drovers.'

Cav said gravely: 'Bo and Billy never really looked happy ploughing.'

This time Mr. Kane's laugh came out faster and louder. 'You only camped with this youngster one night, Cav? He talks like you already.'

Cav picked up his tattered wool hat and the men picked up their big grey felts, and the three of them went down the inside stairs and through the lobby. Cav's legs ached from keeping up with the long-legged Texans, but he felt proud and manly to be with them; nobody on the street looked better, or more at home in the world.

The high-heeled boots started echoes in the Goin' West alley. The men lounged along, not seeming to notice anything, but Cav saw that when they passed a good horse in a stall, both pair of legs hesitated for just a second.

Bo and Billy were still lying down on the piles of straw the stable had provided. Cav picked the goad from the wagon seat, and they both stood up. He said: 'Let me yoke in and show you how they pull. There's not a penny's difference in their walks.'

'Better take him to Kansas with you,' Mr. Kane said. 'He'll do to talk to those mean old buyers at the railhead.'

He laughed, but Big Cav was serious. 'They pulled you from Alabama without getting footsore,' he said. 'That's good enough for me. It's the wagon, Jeff, I want you to look over.' He climbed up in the seat, tugged at the bows. 'Stout and neat. A little heavy, but we're not aiming to use mules. Just what we want, it seems to me. Chuck box and the water barrel in the back; two more just behind the seat; and the bedrolls and tarps go in the middle. It'll be like riding the Pullmans to Kansas.'

Mr. Kane said: 'Good oxen like these can walk ahead of any Texas steers, if you grain them up; and there's room in that wagon for three months' barley for two head. I say buy, and be glad later. Three hundred?'

Big Cav shrugged. 'We can do better than that. Three hundred and twenty-five, all right, Cav?'

Cav said: 'It's a lot of money. What do I do with the furniture?'

Big Cav said: 'Oh.'

Cav went and started undoing the tiedowns on the wagon cover. He stripped them back to show them Maw's rocker and her cherrywood dresser and the rest of the things she had prized too much to leave in Alabama.

Big Cav said: 'That sure isn't the gear to take to Kansas.'

Cav said: 'You keep talking about Kansas, but I thought you were all Texans.'

Jeff Kane said: 'That we are, though I was born right here in Louisiana. My mother's kinfolks are all over the state, French people, though it doesn't show much on me. But I left when I wasn't much taller than you. . . . Texas cattle drovers, that's us, me and Cav. We buy beef in Texas and spend the summer driving it to the railroads in Kansas. Thirty-five hundred this year. All beef stuff, too, no cows.'

Cav said, at once: 'Bo and Billy go best for me. I was there when Paw broke them to yoke, two years ago. They've never slept more than a hundred feet from me in their lives.'

Jeff Kane said: 'What'd I tell you? Boy could sell rain-water in Houston.'

Big Cav said: 'Now, here's what's the trouble. You're rich, Cav. Don't imagine any boy in this town has three hundred and twenty-five dollars.'

'Rich man can't drive a cook wagon,' Mr. Kane said.

'It wouldn't be fitting. And, like the fellow asked, if you're so rich, why aren't you smart?'

'There's something wrong with that,' Big Cav said.

'What I'm trying to say is, Cav here ought to go to school. I've got cousins here will store the furniture for you, kid. And for a hundred dollars a year, old Professor Lovatt'll feed, sleep, and educate you to a fare-thee-well.'

Cav looked from one tall man to the other. He felt hemmed in by a living forest. He said: 'I want to go up the trail with you.'

'When you finish school,' Big Cav said.

'School's almost over for the year.'

'At least two months more at Professor Lovatt's,' Mr. Kane said.

'Is that the school you ran away from?'

Big Cav started laughing, and then so did Mr. Kane. It seemed hopeful for a moment, but then Big Cav stopped laughing, and so did the other man.

Big Cav said: 'I'm going to put it this way, and then shut up and leave it to you, Cav. If your folks were here, what would they tell you to do?'

Cav felt his face getting red. He started to say that that wasn't fair fighting, but he knew it would sound weak and childish. He finally said: 'All right.'

'You've got all your life to punch cattle in,' Big Cav said. 'And here's your money. Man that's old enough to make up his own mind is old enough to hold his own bankroll.'

Jeff Kane said: 'Cav can drive your furnishings around to my Cousin Rachel to store. Enough cousins there to help him unload three ox carts. I'll lead the way to the professor's.'

'You're in a mighty hurry to get me penned in,' Cav said.

Big Cav nodded. 'Grass is on the prairie; sooner we start our drive, the more time we have to get into trouble.'

3

Now it was very hot in the little room up under the eaves of Professor Lovatt's big house. The doctor had gone, after being convinced by Cav's yells that he really had a stomach-ache.

Cav slid out of the bed, and out of the nightgown, and started shucking into his clothes. He had tried, and had tried hard. But Latin and plane geometry didn't seem to connect with cattle-driving, and the other boys laughed at his efforts to learn the French that came so naturally to them. They laughed, too, at the way he talked, so different from the sugar-coated words that poured out of their throats. And it was hot, and joining the school so late in the year he was out of everything and. . . .

Somewhere west of the Sabine and then north, Big Cav was on the trail, and he could find him. And if he couldn't get a job, he'd just trail along for his food, helping the cook if they wouldn't let him drive cattle or a wagon.

He just couldn't stand it here! He had tried, but it was no good. Surely Big Cav would understand.

The school was at a soccer game out in the big pasture. He wrapped his two hundred-odd dollars in a handkerchief, buttoned it carefully into his hip pocket, and pulled on his old wool hat.

Somehow, it seemed dishonest to take the new clothes he had had to buy for going to class and Sunday school and all. But he might need them. He was leaving the Professor the hundred dollars tuition and board and room money, anyway; three weeks had not made much of a dent in it.

The demmies, as the boys called the women who did the housework, were busy on the ground floor. He tiptoed past the room they were cleaning, and was out in the warm, wet Louisiana air.

Nobody noticed him, a raggedy boy with his good clothes inside his bedroll, as he walked downtown. He sure didn't look like one of Professor Lovatt's young gentlemen.

I wish them luck, Cav thought. *I wish them all the luck in the world, but their way is not for me.*

He went past the two livery stables and the wagon yard and the hotel, and clear down and across the river.

In a big field flags were flying and a brass band was playing, and this was where he was headed: a livestock auction.

The boom of the auctioneer's voice and the rap of his gavel could be heard before he was across the bridge. Supposing all the good saddle horses were sold!

A pair of oxen, black and as big as Bo and Billy, were on the block when he got there. Maybe that was a sign of luck, because he sure aimed to see Bo and Billy—see them and maybe drive them again—before he was much taller.

The price they went for filled him with shame. Seems like Big Cav had paid him twice what his outfit was worth, so as to put him into school. But Big Cav had said it was the Pennsylvania-made wagon he was after, that good, strong wagons were hard to come by.

No wagons were on sale at this yard.

Cav circulated around, quietly, looking at the horses. A bright buckskin held his eye for a moment, until he noticed that the horse stood hip-shot, all right, as a smart horse should rest, but that he never shifted; favoured his off-hind leg. A horse with two good hind legs took turns letting each one out of joint, while the other carried the weight.

There was a bay mare, awfully nice looking. A man was leading her around, limbering her up. Broad at the withers, and big in the nostrils, sturdy all over except below the hocks, where she daintied out as pretty as you'd want.

Cav laid his bedroll down and put on his poor-boy smile. 'Lead her around for you, mister?'

'Sho.' This was another Louisiana voice. 'Give you a nickel. She's restless to be going, with all this stock around.'

As soon as he picked up the rope, Cav knew this was for him. Cowboys didn't much fancy mares, he knew, but that was for working cattle; a mare was a little skittish for rope work. But he was buying this one for a road horse, a travelling horse, Big Cav had called it, and this mare would really eat miles.

But then he turned, and saw that, tied to a picket line not far away, was the mare's double. Same colour, same height, same everything.

27

Too bad. Here in fancy Alexandria, a matched team was the ambition of all the hoity-toity society. They would pay big money for such, out of his class. And he didn't need two horses, anyway; his bedroll and he were no great burden. He said: 'Want me to walk the other mare, too, mister?'

The seller was lounging on the ground, in the shade of the tethered mare. 'Nope. 'Tain't necessary. Restlessness just ain't in her. What is, is clumsiness, stumblingness, and a sort of general no-goodness.'

Cav stared at the mare on the tether-line, the mare at the other end of the halter rope he held. 'You can't tell them apart.'

'Nope. Man who sold 'em to me said they was sisters, a year apart. Good one's the older. Nature moves in a wondrous way, to confound a man. Reckon I'll get mebbe a hundred dollars for the five-year-old; and anybody waving, say, a ten or eleven dollar bill under my nose can take the four-year one. Ain't it marvellous?'

His eyes closed, and he drowsed, only his jaw moving slowly, his lips occasionally puckering to spit.

Cav walked the five-year-old until a clerk came and slapped number-stickers on the two mares' rumps and led them away to the sales ring. Their owner woke up and stood up, all in one motion, and handed Cav the promised nickel.

The auction moved as fast as a mountain stream. A buggy horse—'Goes single, goes double, he does it all!' was being bid on when Cav got to the ring. He wriggled between adult legs and grounded buggy whips and got to the front row. The auctioneer chanted: 'Sixty-five, do I hear seventy, once? Sixty-five, will you raise, twice! Sixty-five, and sold to Shawnee, three times and out!'

The peddler to whom Cav had given a ride, came forward and took the horse's halter. The horse was a grey, big-

28

hoofed and bulky, but well-nostrilled and deep in the chest.

Shawnee was paying up at the desk. The clerk led the gawky four-year-old in, and started around the ring with her. No question; she was as clumsy as a bear in double harness. Maybe she'd had the rheumatiz when she was a filly; each of her joints bent like it was encased in dry rawhide.

A couple of men laughed. The auctioneer loosed his awesome voice: 'I'll say this for her; she's g'aranteed agin runaways!' There was more laughter. 'So I hear twenty-five, twenty-five, twenty-five? Couldn't be a more gentle hoss in all Louisian'! Do I hear twenty, twenty, twenty, she is young, and she'll never wear herself out! Do I hear fifteen,

fifteen, fifteen, is there a preacher in the crowd wants a saddle hoss won't disturb his Bible-readin'? Do I hear ten, ten, ten, she is a bargain and——'

Shawnee said: 'Ten.'

'Ten from the amiable Shawnee, and what man has ever known him to be worsted in a bargain? Ten I have, ten I have, and do I hear fifteen? Ten I have, ten is bid, and let me hear twelve! I have ten, ten, ten, ten, how about ten and four bits? Then going once to Shawnee for ten, twice at ten, do I hear a bid? Three times and she is sold, sold to Shawnee for ten dollars, please pay the clerk.'

The clerk led in the fast-walking five-year-old and started leading her about. There was a wave of noise from the crowd, and men threw down their cigars, leaned forward to see better. Cav had to struggle to hold his place.

The auctioneer took up the ancient chant: 'Ain't she neat, ain't she sweet, hear the click of her dainty feet! A beauty, gentlemen, a beauty, five years old and solid as a dollar, will do to go double, loves to go single, and an angel under the saddle! She'll do to go to Californy, or down to the corner meeting house, she'll swim all the rivers and climb all the mountains and stand quiet in front of the grocery store, that's what she'll do. A beauty, a princess, and the pride of Louisian'! Do I hear seventy-five, do I hear seventy-five, you'll not hurt her feelings by bidding less. Do I hear——'

'Seventy-five,' Shawnee said.

'Eighty-five,' Cav said.

There was not exactly silence; that never occurred in such a crowd of tobacco-spitting men. But there was some quiet. The auctioneer spoke in his kitchen rather than his auction-ring voice. 'Now, young man, mind yourself! We're talking money, not marbles or chalk.'

30

Cav unbuttoned his hip pocket, took out the folded handkerchief, showed his bills.

The auctioneer stared. 'You a runaway, son? You been dabbling in your master's till?'

Unexpectedly, the owner of the Goin' West Livery Stable thrust out of the crowd. 'His money, I reckon. He sold a span and an oxcart to Cavanagh, the trail-drover, couple of weeks ago.'

The auctioneer coughed into a red bandana and nodded. 'Since he's vouched for by an old customer and an old friend, let's get on with this. I've got eighty-five, eighty-five, eighty-five from—what's your name, son?'

'Don't matter,' Cav said.

'And you know horse-flesh like you deserved the name, and that's a fact. Mr. Don't Matter bids eighty-five, eighty-five, eighty-five, and do I hear ninety?'

'Ninety,' Shawnee said.

'Ninety from Shawnee the Peddler, and do I hear a hundred, a hundred, a——'

'A hundred,' Cav said.

'Hundred from the little sport, and do I hear a hundred and a quarter, hundred and a——'

Shawnee's thin face was twisted. Like he was dying, he groaned: 'Hundred-five.'

'Hundred-five, hundred-five, hundred-five. I shouldn't take less than ten dollar jumps on this beauty, but let it go, do I hear——'

'One hundred and twenty-five,' Cav said.

The auctioneer shot a look at him, and then shrugged. The chant started: 'Hundred and a quarter, hundred and . . . .'

Opposite him Shawnee took out an old wallet, untied it, unclasped it, unfolded it. He slid some bills out, held them close to his greasy shirt, and counted. He put the bills in his side pocket, pressed an elbow over it, and counted his coins. Then he turned away and disappeared into the crowd.

The auctioneer cried the price three times, and the mare was Cav's. He went to pay the clerk, the auctioneer forgetting to chant as he watched out of the corner of one eye. The clerk took the money, counted it twice, nodded, the chant started again, and Cav led his mare out of the ring.

He discovered her name was Belle. It would go well with Bo and Billy when he caught up with Big Cav.

The man who had sold the mares was still by the picket-line. 'Here's your bedroll all safe, and you bought yourself a pretty, pretty piece of hoss' flesh. You plan to drive or ride her?'

'Ride her,' Cav said.

'She'll do either, handy as fallin' into a barrel of whisky.' It was pretty plain that the tobacco-chewer had not expected the price he had gotten. 'If you need you a saddle, there's a fellow yonder brought in a wagon-load, second-hand, but lots of them good enough. Offer half what he asks, and split the difference.'

'Thanks.' Cav started to hand over the lead rope, thought better of it, and wriggled up on Belle's back.

'That's right,' the seller said. 'Yo're a hoss owner now. No need to walk.'

Cav rode over to the saddler's wagon. He wasn't heavy, and he didn't know how to rope, and even if he did, Belle would never make a roping horse; she was for travelling. There were ten and fifteen dollar saddles there, and they would have done fine to carry a boy and his bedroll. But he paid forty dollars for a tree covered with rawhide and a heavy Mexican roping horn, big as a saucer on top, a real roping saddle.

32

'The steer hasn't ben raised that can bust that saddle,' the man said. 'She'd hold a seven-year-old bull. . . . Want to buy a real linen throwing rope? Five dollars.'

Cav had no idea what a rope was worth, but the man had priced his saddles fairly. He tied the rope to the saddle's pigging strings, the handy clumps of rawhide thongs that a man could cut off to hog-tie a cow or mend a fence, or anything else, rode back to the picket-line and heaved his bedroll aboard. The man who sold Belle helped him tie it down evenly.

Then he headed out for the West, for the Sabine River and Texas. On the edge of town he passed Shawnee.

The peddler was riding a buggy whose wheels wobbled a little at each turn. Maybe they just needed soaking in a stream, but this was damp country. Shawnee ought to see a wheel-wright.

Ahead, Belle's sister and the big-footed grey plodded along. Cav reined Belle in alongside. 'Hello, Mr. Shawnee.'

Shawnee surely had heard him come up. But he raised his head and said: 'Oh. You.'

'Sorry about bidding against you, but I've got a long way to go, and this mare looked like the only thing there that could take me fast and sure.'

Shawnee said: 'Step off your saddle and ride sitting awhile.'

'I've got a long way to go. . . . Just wanted to be sure there were no hard feelings.'

Shawnee had let his head fall down again. 'That's all right. Just that I wanted to match the mares. They'd look nice together.'

'No match,' Cav said. 'Your mare would never keep up with Belle.'

'Belle, eh? Belle. Not a bad name for a mare. . . .'

'Don't see what you need three horses for, anyway. You already had bought the grey.'

The deep-set eyes bored into Cav's. 'You don't miss much do you?' Cav picked up his reins.

Then Shawnee smiled. 'Maybe we'll meet up the road again,' he said. 'For all your mare's so clean-footed and fast. Name of Belle, eh?'

'That's right.'

'Good-bye till then, son,' Shawnee's head went down and he seemed to sleep. In the back of the buggy his peddler's pack loomed large.

Cav said: 'Good luck,' and rode on, not knowing why he felt so queer.

34

4

HE was two and a half days more in Louisiana. Then he and Belle crossed the Sabine, and there was Texas.

Cav didn't know what he'd expected to see, but this wasn't it. The west bank of the Sabine was just like the east bank, for all he could tell. Still, camping that night, eating bacon and beans and drinking tea, he thought: that noise is Belle chewing Texas grass, and later he slept with a smile on his face.

They were covering about thirty miles a day, he figured. His day was well planned. In the morning, he put the beans, that had soaked all night, on the fire while he cooked himself some bacon; at noon he made another fire and cooked the beans some more; at night they were ready to eat before the sun was down. Now, in spring, wild onions were plentiful on the prairie, and he put some in his beans, cut up raw, as his Maw had taught him.

He seldom thought about his family now, or about Big Cav and Mr. Kane ahead. It was like he was hung up like the sun over the prairie, coming from no place, going no place, just covering his piece of ground every day.

When he could, he rode around towns, but when beans and bacon began to choke him, he'd go in and have maybe a fried steak or a few eggs in some little inn, talking to no one but the person who waited on him, man or woman, chewing his food and swallowing and riding again.

More often he would just buy a can of tomatoes at a cross-roads store and eat it out on the trail while Belle munched bought oats off her saddle blanket.

She was as good as he'd thought she would be, and she didn't really need the oats, having plenty of time to eat spring grass and having only to carry a boy and his bed.

If she had a fault—and what horse doesn't?—it was a notion to bite down on the bit when she saw a horse ahead. She had been raced in company, Cav decided, which his father had always said would ruin a travelling horse. But she was young, and as the days wore on and she saw that Cav didn't want to outrun everything on the road, she gave up and settled for a little dancing and head-tossing.

So everything was fine till he rode into the little town of Jasper.

Not that Jasper looked so small to a trail rider. Must be two, three hundred people, Cav thought, to see all at one time. A lot. There were five stores and a jail and an inn with an eating and two sleeping rooms. Bigger than most along the way.

Belle's off-hind shoe needed clinching, and he gave the

36

blacksmith four bits for that, and the rest of a dollar for a pair of bronc shoes to carry in his bedroll. The smith threw in some nails, and Cav had kept his father's shoeing hammer out of the household goods. He had never put a shoe on anything but a quiet ox, but he figured by now Belle knew him so well she'd stand for him.

He would have ridden on, then, but when he came out of the smithy a tall man blocked his way. Cav went to lead around him, but the man sidestepped.

He was wearing a star and a gun and a big hat. He said: 'I'm the sheriff of Jasper County.' He flipped his thumb across the square. 'Got an office in the jail. Want to come sit and talk a minute?'

The way he put it, it was hardly a question. Cav led Belle across and tied her to the jailhouse hitching rail. He loosened her cinch a little, and patted her nose before following the sheriff.

The lawman said: 'Nice mare. What do you call her?'

It must be peaceful country for the sheriff to have so much time to waste on things like that. But it was silly not to be polite to the man with the star; Cav said: 'Her name's Belle.'

The sheriff said: 'Ahhhh,' like this seemed to make him happy. 'You name her?'

'She was called that when I got her.'

The sheriff said: 'Ahhhhh,' again. 'Where was that, son?'

'Alexandria, Lou'siana.'

'You better come in the office and sit a spell.'

The office wasn't much; a match-board shelter pinned on the front of the stone cell-block. But there was a desk, and a chair behind the desk, and a bench. Cav sat on the bench and looked at the yellow Wanted notices on the wall. Some of them seemed so old the sheriff could have taken

them down; the wanted criminals were surely beyond the
age of making trouble for the law.

The papers the law officer took out of the single drawer
of his desk were whiter and newer. The sheriff rustled
through them, wetting his thumb from time to time.

Cav read a paper in a frame on the wall that said that
Henry J. Eppes was Sheriff of Jasper County.

'Here y'are,' the sheriff said. 'Now listen. Appeared before me, a Justice of the Peace for—you don't need all that—one Homer C. Davis—ha, boy?—who hereby states that a certain juvenile—described in law as an infant, being of the age of thirteen years approximately—named Johnny Robinson—being legally and under fee bonded to said Homer C. Davis—did escape, run away and decamp from the person of said Homer C. Davis—and did purloin, steal and take away one valuable mare, a bay, rising five years old, of the name of Belle—fourteen hands, two inches, herein described—hnnnh, boy? What you got to say?'

Cav said: 'My name is Cavalier Rand, Mr. Eppes.'

'Huh? My name's Smith, boy. Why call me by that fat-head Eppes's name?'

Cav looked at the framed paper on the wall. His stomach was cold; he was licked and he knew it. Who was going to believe a boy? When a real Justice of the Peace had sworn out a paper? . . .

'Must take that down some time,' Sheriff Smith said. 'I drubbed Eppes good, last election. What you say?'

'I've got a bill-of-sale for the mare. And I've never been bonded to anyone.'

The sheriff shoved his hat back on his head. He scratched the low forehead that this exposed. If the people of Jasper County preferred him to Mr. Eppes, Cav thought, Eppes must have been a lulu. 'It says that here,' Smith said. 'That your master, Mr. Davis, is a horse trader, and that you stole a bill-of-sale blank, have filled it out and pretend to own the mare, fair and square.'

'I do.' But it sounded weak, even to Cav. Who had done this to him, and why?

Sheriff Smith got red in the face. He rapped the white paper. 'Now, this is a legal paper, all made out in a peace court. You asking me to believe that a boy like you, little

39

raggedy-shirt-tail kid, has money to buy that kind of hoss-flesh? The sheriffs down the line must be a measly lot to let you get this far. This paper came in a couple of days ago, on the railroad, from up north. I get mail by the railroad all the time, being sheriff.'

Cav felt very, very tired. 'I was travelling with my family, and they died,' he said. 'A man named Bruce Cavanagh bought the family oxen and so on from me, and I bought the mare.'

'Belle,' Sheriff Smith said. 'You admit her name is Belle.'

'Yes, but I bought her.'

'Illegal,' the sheriff said. 'After a deceasement, property must be held for a year for the proper settlement of accounts and so on. It's called probate.' He cleared his throat. 'No mistake, boy. This paper is all fair and legal. I oughta know, being sheriff. . . . I'll send a message to the railroad at Livingston and they'll wire Alexandria, and pretty soon your master, this Mister Davis'll show up and pay my costs and take you into his legal custody. Maybe he'll even pay me a reward, seein' the fine mare I'm getting back for him.'

'Yes,' Cav said.

'You gotta stay in the jail here. The mare'll go to the livery stable. It all goes on the county's costs against Mr. Davis.'

'Be sure and feed Belle well,' Cav said. 'I've been getting her oats and corn when I could.'

'Feed you and the mare both,' Sheriff Smith said. 'I am a fair and square man. The county thought so, or I wouldn't be sheriff.'

Cav asked: 'Which cell do I take?'

'Any one you want,' the sheriff said, waving a large hand at the block. 'Just make yourself at home. We don't get many prisoners here.'

He sounded regretful about it.

40

5

THE cell wasn't bad, and the sheriff was right; there were no other prisoners in the week that Cav spent as his guest. Wasn't much law business, either, it seemed, because after Sheriff Smith found out that Cav played checkers, they spent most of their daylight hours doing just that.

When Cav gave the sheriff his promise not to run away, they took to going to the officer's home to eat their meals. Mrs. Smith wasn't much brighter than her husband, but she could cook pretty well; if Cav had had his freedom, it wouldn't have been a bad week at all.

But it was hard to be penned up here in Jasper, with Big Cav getting farther and farther north all the time. And there was the worry about what was going to happen when this Mr. Homer C. Davis showed up.

Cav kept wondering who he could be; he couldn't think of anyone who'd go to all that trouble to bother a boy and steal a mare, even a fine one like Belle.

The person Mr. Davis turned out to be was Shawnee, the peddler. Looking over the checkerboard and past the sheriff and out the single window in the office, Cav saw him pull up one morning, stiff-legged mare, big-footed grey, buggy, pack and all, and at once Cav knew this must be the man who had lawyered him down.

He was almost glad to see Shawnee, he was so sick of beating Sheriff Smith at checkers.

Shawnee said: 'Sheriff, I am Homer C. Davis, known as Shawnee the Peddler.'

Sheriff Smith shoved his hat back. 'This the boy, Mr. Davis?'

'That's him, all right,' Shawnee said. 'You rascal, when I've been so good to you!'

Cav didn't bother to answer. If not arguing would get him out of jail, he wasn't going to argue.

'Where's my mare?' Shawnee asked. 'Where's Belle?'

'In the town livery stable,' Sheriff Smith said. 'You owe for her bill. And for the boy's meals. An' my costs for catching him for you.'

'I'm a poor man,' Shawnee said. 'I make my living peddling from house to house as I travel the roads of Texas. How much does it come to?'

The sheriff said twenty dollars. Shawnee said he could pay ten. Cav thought he'd go crazy, sitting in that splintery office, with the whole world just outside the window. The sheriff had never searched him, and he still had money. He almost offered to pay the difference, but finally the sheriff took fourteen dollars from Shawnee, and they were outside.

'Sit in the buggy,' the peddler said. 'I'll go get my mare.'

Your mare, Cav thought. My mare, Belle. But he kept his mouth shut. The jail was still right there, and the jail office, and Sheriff Smith. So Cav slung his bedroll in the back, next to the peddler's pack, and sat down on the left side of the buggy seat.

Some fat man had owned that rig once, because the right-hand side was all sprung down from carrying a big driver. Shawnee's scraggly frame had never done it, certainly not in the time since Alexandria.

Then Shawnee came out of the livery stable leading Belle, with Cav's saddle cinched on her back. She had her halter on under her spade-bit bridle. Shawnee tied her to the tail

42

of the buggy, and climbed over the wheel. He took the reins up and clucked to Belle's sister and the grey, and they started off.

Cav noticed that the wheels didn't wobble as bad as they had. Shawnee must have spent a little money with a wheel-wright.

They passed the houses of Jasper, close together first and then sprawled apart to make room for cotton land, and Belle danced at the end of her halter rope, glad to be on the road again.

'Texas doesn't look much different from Louisiana,' Cav said.

'This is East Texas. Wait'll you see the central part, where the cattle are. . . . I've never been across the Pecos, but they say it is all wild, mountains and pine trees and big wild cattle, like buffalo. That was a mighty dirty trick I played on you, boy.'

Cav said: 'Yes, it was.'

'Maybe I'll be sorry some day. But I had to do it. I needed that mare badly.'

'Now that you've got her, why don't you ride her or let me ride her? She's too good to be treated that way, led behind a buggy.'

Shawnee clucked to the slow-moving team. They stumbled into a trot, but then at once fell back to their plodding walk. 'Easy, boy, easy,' Shawnee said, not to the horses. 'Why, if you got on that mare, you'd be over the hills and far away, and then how would I find you?'

'That's right,' Cav said. 'The sheriff in the next town you wrote to might not be as stupid as Smith.'

'Easy, easy. Wasn't you brought up to be respectable to and about your elders? Why, now you think maybe that I did you a dirty trick, and maybe I did—Shawnee doesn't fool himself—but I'll make it up to you. You and me's going to be partners, boy, real partners. Rich ones, too.'

'No, thanks.'

'Now, don't be hasty, boy, don't be hasty. We'll stop at this house; betcha a million the lady'll be wanting thread or needles or maybe a nice new saucepan. You carry the pack.'

'No.'

Shawnee pulled the reins and the horses stopped, their noses against a white picket fence. 'Ain't you learned?' he asked. 'Don't you know the way the world wags, boy? There's nobody gonna take your word against mine, a droop-nosed kid against a man growed. Better do like I say, boy. Fighting's not gonna get your mare back, and if you don't work, you don't eat.'

'Your food would choke my throat.'

'Temper, temper,' Shawnee said. He sighed again, and clucked to his team to start up. He had to slap them with the reins to get the message to them. 'Well, one day more or less won't matter. I'm a poor man and peddling is a poor trade, and I don't make so much in a day but what I can't afford to give up one afternoon's profit. By tomorrow, you'll be hungry enough to do like I say.'

'No.'

The dust rose on their wheels and dropped into the road again. The mare and the grey switched their tails against flies. Behind the buggy Belle danced, restlessly.

Shawnee said: 'We'll see, we'll see. But you can see, when I've gone to all this trouble, spent money on your board bill and the mare's, not to mention the original complaint and the Justice of the Peace's fees, and all, I can't leave you alone to steal that mare from me again.'

'Steal! I bought Belle with my own money, that I got for selling Paw's oxen and his wagon and——'

44

'Now, sonny, I feel real bad about this already. Don't make it worse by crying, and we'll make out jest dandy.'

They camped that night by a river that Shawnee thought was maybe the Neches. There was wood and water to spare. Shawnee watered the grey and Belle, leaving Belle's sister to stiff-leg down to the river and back by herself. Then he opened his foodbox and took out a big pepper-box pistol that he tucked into his belt. Sitting on the food-box, he built him a little fire; then he stood up and got out dried beef and a bottle of little peppers, some real onions and a saucepan and made himself a supper.

He didn't bother to offer to feed Cav, and Cav didn't ask. He went and got his saddle, where Shawnee had dumped it off Belle's back, and his bedroll and made himself up on the ground and turned in, empty-bellied, before full dark had settled.

When he woke up, the Big Dipper said it was close to midnight. He slid from his blankets as quiet as he knew how, pulled on his boots. Then he shuffled his feet over to where the peddler lay by the almost-dead fire.

No good. Shawnee had Belle's tie rope twisted around his upper arm.

There wasn't a knife in the world sharp enough to cut that rope without waking the peddler up.

No good. Cav went back to his bed and sat on it, his knees under his chin. There was nothing he could do. A boy alone, in strange country—maybe he had even broken some law in running away from school. Maybe a boy had to learn Latin and algebra and all to steer clear of the law.

No good.

The stiff-legged mare and the grey were down towards the river, grazing. A saddle blanket under Belle's nose

D

showed that Shawnee had grained her, for which Cav was thankful. . . . If he left her with Shawnee, at least she wouldn't be starved or mistreated. The peddler seemed to set store by her.

Clouds were scudding across the moon. Cav rolled his bedroll again, his good clothes still in the middle. He wished he could get some food, if only cornmeal, to take along; hard times ahead. But no hope.

He carried the bedroll down to the river-bank, left it there. The stiff mare and the grey looked at him, kind of soft-like; full of good river grass, they were quiet and sleepy.

His saddle came next. Better not use it just yet.

The bridles were hung on the pole of the buggy where it pointed at the western sky. Somewhere he'd heard—his Paw? Big Cav?—that a smart traveller always points his wagon pole the way he wants to go tomorrow, lest fog come up in the night.

Shawnee was a smart enough traveller. Too smart. Too smart a traveller, too smart all the way around.

When Cav's fingers felt over the bridles, the peddler turned a little in his sleep, and Belle went back on her halter rope. Cav crouched behind the buggy while Shawnee raised his head, looked around, said: 'There, girl, there,' to Belle, and went back to sleep again.

Belle dropped her head and snorted.

No time to rebuckle a bridle, to fit the cheekstraps and all to the size of a horse's head. Cav felt carefully till he was sure he had the right one. The grey's head was a lot longer than that of either of the mares; he was a real pulling horse, not fine-boned like they were. Once in a while a buckle would clink or a chain would jingle as Cav loosened the bridle from the rest of the outfit.

46

When he was sure, he unbuckled it from the buggy harness, thankful at least that it didn't have blinders. He'd cut the lines to saddle size some time later. His pocket knife was all right, but it could do with a sharpening, and that would make noise.

He slid down to the river-bank again. The stiff-legged mare was lying down, but the grey stood near her. He slid up on the horse, slid the bridle over his head. Night was warm, no need to hold the bit in his hand first.

The grey blew gently down his neck. Blanket went on easy, saddle thumped a little, then the bedroll. Balance it just

so, walk around to the offside to tie down, don't take any chances of galling the horse's back.

'So, Grey,' he whispered. 'So, Grey.' It was as good a name as any for a horse he had no feelings for.

Cinch up good, bringing up his knee to force the air out of the grey's belly. Grey didn't mind; he'd been under saddle before. If he hadn't Cav would have had himself a time. Should have thought of that sooner; he'd been lucky.

He slid into Grey's saddle like a ghost sitting on a thin cloud, coiled the clumsy buggy lines into his left hand, and sunk his heels.

He followed the river way downstream before he dared to cross. The stiff mare followed all the way.

When he went into the water she stood hesitating, and Cav flicked her nose with the end of his long line, and she turned back. He could maybe make better time with a second horse to shift to, but he'd look like a horse stealer.

Maybe he was, in the eyes of such as Sheriff Smith. But he was leaving Belle, and she was worth three of the big-footed Grey.

The water in the Neches wasn't much more than belly-deep. Cav pulled his boots up to the withers, and kept them dry, and then Grey was wading out, and the clouds were still scudding from west to east, but he was on the west bank of the Neches, and on his way.

6

IT was a long and hungry journey. Towns would have sheriffs in them, and maybe Shawnee had found himself another Justice of the Peace and another paper saying Cav was a horse thief. So, no towns.

Sometimes he ate at farm houses, and later at ranch houses, paying out of his money. Then he came to the cow country and there were line camps and round-up camps, where the cook wouldn't take his money, or even let him wash up afterwards; in cow country food didn't amount to a thing, and a strange face was something everybody wanted to see. But even so, he missed as many meals as he ate, the camps were so far apart.

By now everybody had heard of Kane and Cavanagh, and he pretty well knew where to find them; they'd headed out of the holding grounds north of San Antone, maybe a month ago, and would be well up the trail.

'Figger a cow-trailin's outfit can go maybe fifteen miles

a day,' one old line camp boss said. 'Figger a hoss can go thirty miles, twice that. You'll catch them, son.'

He turned his eyes away from Grey, politely.

Truth was, Grey was no more of a travelling horse than Cav had taken him for. He didn't stumble, and he wasn't stiff in the knees or windbroken, but those big feet took forever to pick themselves up and put themselves down again. A cook in a division camp said he had once shoed horses at a racetrack, and tried to cut the big streaked hooves down to a handier size, but it hardly helped at all.

That man wouldn't take money for the new shoes. 'Running-W buys shoes by the boatload, son. They come ashore at Matagorda, or maybe Corpus Chris'. They got no need for your money.'

This was cow country, open and rolling and green and full of fine men. Cav had made no mistake in running away from Alex, in swimming the Neches, in missing the meals he'd had to miss; this was what he had hoped for, this was what he had come for.

Nights he'd throw his rope at a huisache bush or a rock, and he was getting so it would settle where he wanted it to, every time.

In late June, he spotted three riders nooning over a little fire, and rode up to them. They filled his tin cup and his tin plate, and munched gravely while they watched to see if he liked cold cornpone and hot bacon fat. He did.

He said: 'Anything I can do to pay for my grub?' He'd learned it was the thing to say, though there never was.

The tallest cowboy had said his name was Dun Maguire. 'Naw, Cav. We were just sent back from the tail end of the herd, what we call the drag, to cut out strays that drifted off to the ranch herds around here. We've got a little bunch of them up ahead in a nice grassy draw. No use eating with a cow in your lap if you don't have to.'

'Know whether Kane and Cavanagh are ahead of you? I'm trying to catch up with K and C.'

'I wondered about that name of yours,' Dun said. 'Kin to Big Cav, eh? Yeah, they're ahead of us, a half day's ride or less. We ride for Mike and Harry Grolier.'

It was like he had come home; though this wasn't a homey kind of spot, exactly. There were some rocks, some cactus, and a great deal of the Spanish bayonet, and that was it. But those cows bawling over the swell were trail cows, and the noise they made was a friendly noise.

Cav said: 'I'll help you drive your stragglers up.'

Dun Maguire looked at Grey without any expression crossing his face at all. 'Can always use an extra hand,' he said. 'You'n me'll ride right flank, out on the prairie, and I'll put a boy between the critters and the line of rocks, and a man to ride drag, and we'll move out like we had tickets on the steam cars.'

Cav felt his face getting red: 'I guess at that, old Grey there couldn't do much towards turning a real steer. He certainly isn't a cow pony.'

'Well,' Dun said, 'not if the steer had made his mind up.'

Cav started to tell him about Belle, and about Shawnee and all. Then he choked the words back into his throat and swallowed them. He had an idea of what his Paw would have said about a man on a splay-foot horse who talked big about the handsome roadster he just didn't happen to have with him; and these trail drovers were pretty much like Paw would have been, if Paw hadn't had so many troubles and so much family.

Besides, how did he know word might get to somebody who was a stickler for the law or a hog for rewards, and the paper that Shawnee had sworn out against him maybe might still stand.

Better all around to keep his mouth shut.

It was only a little past noon when they stepped into the saddle and rode up on the knot of straggled cattle Dun had collected; the prickly pear cactus was throwing shadows that just reached past their own edges. Dun pulled a blue bandana over his nose and mouth, and he and Cav rode the dusty plains edge of the little herd; a cowboy with a blue neckcloth rode the rocks; and the one in the rear had wrapped a cotton muffler over his ears and head; drag, riding behind the herd, was a dusty job.

Cav had seen plenty of cattle since he'd gotten into Texas; long-legged, high-bellied steers and cows and some bulls, not at all like the milch breed back in Alabam', or like Bo and Billy, the oxen he'd sold Big Cav and Mr. Kane. He'd seen those Texas cows munching rank grass in the river bottoms, or browsing mesquite beans off the little trees that dotted the uplands; but he hadn't seen them under drive and on the trail.

Now he knew why they were built the way they were. Those animals could walk as fast as a good horse, and feed themselves as they went, head down, snatch a mouthful of grass, head up and chew and swallow it.

The cowmen didn't push them, just let the animals take their own time and their own path, so long as it was north and towards the main herd and Kansas. When a cow or a steer tried to turn back, there was a cowboy and a pony in his way, not doing much, maybe the rider slapping a hand down on his leather chaps, maybe not even that. Same if a cow wanted to go up in the rocks or out on the prairie; there was always somebody right in his way.

So the little herd went north.

It was dusty work. Cav didn't have a neckerchief, but he reached into his pants and pulled out his shirt-tail and cut off a good, generous chunk of it with his clasp knife and made himself a nose and chin covering like the other riders.

That was a help.

Up till now, Dun had been chowsing his cow pony right along (the Texas word for making an animal move fast), stepping in front of every cow that sought to wander to the side. But here came one, not right at Cav, but maybe thirty feet ahead of him, a big steer, black striped down the back and dirty cream for the rest of him.

Cav picked up the reins on Grey's buggy-horse bridle, and swung his legs so his spurless heels clunked into Grey's ribs, and the big-foot picked himself up into a clumsy lope and Cav placed him right in the steer's path.

The steer dropped his head and blew dust, like he could go right through them if he had a mind to, but then turned back into the herd and nosed himself north again, chop, chop, his long tongue twisting at the grass, his sharp teeth nipping it off.

Dun Maguire was probably grinning under his bandana, but he raised his right hand and waved it at Cav like Cav had done the right thing, and it was a good sight to see.

The prickly pear shadows were long when they came on something else to see, and a strange sight it was.

A man came walking south, in this country where no man walked, and he stumbled as he came. Even from a distance Cav could see that he was in trouble, and he forced old Gray to a lope to go help.

But Dun Maguire cut his fast pony in front of Grey and stopped Cav. 'Leave it alone,' he said. His easy-going manner was gone, his voice hardened. 'Let it ride.'

53

'There's a man out there,' Cav said. 'He looks like he's out of water, or sick.'

'Yep,' Dun said. 'He's out of water, and he's probably plenty sick by now, and what's more he doesn't have any boots on.'

Cav stared. Water and boots in this country of sun and cactus were about as important as anything could be.

Dun said, in his new, hard voice: 'Horse-thief. Cav Cavanagh caught him two days ago, trying to sneak a horse out of their remuda.'

'Remuda?'

'Horseherd,' Dun said. He made a flicking gesture with his right hand. 'I'd a hung him, but Cav gave him a chance. If he makes it from waterhole to waterhole, he'll live. If he doesn't, he's one horse-thief less to worry about. . . . Let's get these cows up to Mike and Harry Grolier; I could use some food.'

As they went by the horse-thief, he didn't look up. Cav felt like he was swaying in the saddle, but he wasn't. He hadn't exactly stolen Grey, but there wasn't a very good other name to put on what he'd done. . . .

Mike and Harry Grolier turned out to be smooth-faced, dark-haired brothers from Louisiana, still in their twenties. Dun introduced Cav to Mike, who was gulping coffee at the tailgate of the chuck wagon, and Mike waved a hand at his brother, helping the night wrangler bed down the horses.

Dun Maguire said: 'Thanks a lot for the help,'—though Cav had not done much—and rode ahead with his boys to throw the stragglers into the main herd. Mike Grolier looked at Cav over the tin cup, and then down along Grey's front, resting his eyes, finally, on those huge hoofs. He said: 'Well, light down, stranger, and throw your horse into our remuda. Chuck'll be pretty soon.'

Cav stripped the shirt-tail away from his face, and Grolier said, politely: 'Well, now, you're a young one to be out on the prairie.'

'I'm trying to catch up with K and C. There's a chance that Cav Cavanagh might give me a job. I'm Cav Rand.'

'Kin?'

'No. But Big Cav knows I can drive oxen, and he's got some pulling his wagon.'

'So have we,' Mike Grolier said. 'We could put you on.'

55

'Thanks, but I'd like to see Cav.'

Mike said: 'Well, it doesn't matter. Works out real good. We have a K-C horse that drifted back to us, and I'd like to return him before Big Cav takes me for a horse-thief. You can ride him up.'

He laughed, and after a long, long while, Cav forced a polite smile on his face. But he wasn't laughing inside.

7

THE Groliers made him spend the night at their camp. Cav was glad enough for the rest, though the talk took a turn he didn't care for; the horse-thief had walked clear through the Grolier herd that day, and first one man and then another commented on it, or told stories about what had happened to other horse-thieves, other places.

Cav was glad when full dark came, and the men couldn't see that he wasn't laughing when they laughed.

Most of them thought Big Cav had been too light and easy on the thief.

Finally he got the subject changed. He asked: 'What do you do if the cattle stampede?'

'Stompede,' Mike Grolier said. 'Not stamp. This is Texas.' He laughed. 'Haven't heard stampede since I crossed the Sabine, Cav. Why, me, I get out of their way, and call for big brother, here.'

Harry said: 'Now, Mike, I'm not superstitious, but suppose one of our cow-brutes heard you? Cav, don't even whisper stompede where a cow can read your lips.'

'But what do you do if they run?'

Harry said: 'Ride alongside them, slowly turn them back on themselves. But slow. If you get them milling too tight the middle ones go down and are trampled.'

Mike said: 'That's just about it. A big, slow circle. And don't ever, ever shoot a gun in front of them to turn them. I heard of a fool over on the Chisum trail that tried that, and they haven't found his herd yet.'

'I don't even own a gun,' Cav said.

'Well, they're handy if a horse breaks his leg, or if a rattlesnake shows up in front of you. Now, when Harry and I were running loose on the prairie, shirt-tail kids no older than you are now, I mind me one time, I was working as cookie for old John Mott, and Harry was night wrangler.'

Harry said: 'That was the time Mike fooled me. Being older, I had my choice of jobs. The cook had the meanest face I ever did see, but he turned out to be a gem of a man, it was a pleasure to run his chores for him; and old John Mott, who looked kind as a minister at Easter, he loved his cows so—or the money they were going to fetch him—he was up five times a night riding out to see them, and wanting a fresh horse caught every time.'

'Harry got thin as a roadrunner in the spring.'

'Sure. Well, we decided to run away, even if we had promised to stick with the herd clear to the North Pole, if old John Mott couldn't find a good market south of there. Took me some persuading to get Mike to go with me, he had gotten so fond of that sour-faced cook and his sweet-tasting food.'

'Well, we had given our word,' Mike said.

'We had given our word to a mean old purse-squeezer. Man who takes advantage of kids don't deserve to have his word taken seriously. Course, we didn't think we were kids. Thought we were real grown-up men.'

'Nine feet tall and seven feet wide,' Mike said. 'I was somewhat younger than you, Cav, and Harry somewhat older. Show him your grey hair, bub.'

58

Thunder growled, far to the north, and sheet lightning flashed on the sky.

Mike said: 'Cav, you shouldn't have mentioned stompede. You brought on the lightning. Nothing scares cattle more.'

'Shush, Mike,' Harry said. 'We were having an interesting talk. What do you think, Cav, is a boy bound by a man who forces him to give his word?'

Cav knew what they were up to. But they were a Texas mile off the mark.

They thought him a bond-boy, an orphan ordered by a court to work for someone for his keep until he was old enough to go on his own. They were trying to tell him that it was all right with them.

They were the kindest men he'd ever met, these cattle drovers, but they were not kind to horse-thieves. They fed anybody who came along, but they wouldn't even give a swallow of water to a man who took their horses away.

It made sense in this country, where a horse was safety and a livelihood, and the only means of handling thousands of dollars' worth of cow, but it was cold comfort to know it made sense.

He was safe enough for the time being. The Groliers liked him; horse-thief was the last thing they would think him to be.

The lightning flashed again, and then the thunder. Harry looked worried.

Cav said: 'I could help ride the herd tonight. But that Grey of mine's awful clumsy.'

Harry said: 'Tell the night wrangler we'll all want horses up and saddled,' and Mike got up, walked out towards the remuda, grazing on the mesquite grass just beyond the wagon oxen's bedding ground.

'He'll get up the K-C horse for you,' Harry said. 'Let's

bunk down and get what sleep we can.' He rolled and lit a cigarette, and looked at Cav through the glare of the match. 'Mike and I ran away when we were your age. I know what it is to have no one to tell your troubles to.' Then he waited.

But Cav had made up his mind. His troubles with Shawnee were his own, and he was not going to dump any part of them on his friends. He'd leave Grey with the Groliers, to keep in or turn out as they saw fit, but he wouldn't tell them it was a stolen horse, and that way make them criminals with him. . . .

He slipped under the top blanket of his roll, pillowed his head on his rolled-up shirt—his saddle was on the tethered K-C horse—and put one arm over his eyes to shield them from the frequent, close-by flashes.

He dreamed the thunder was getting closer and more frequent, and then Mike was shaking him. 'Roll, roll out, Cav. Hit the saddle!'

'Stompede?'

'Not ours. Cav's, I think. Hear the ground shake?'

While he was talking, Mike was buttoning his shirt. Cav pulled his boots on, got his arms into his own shirt and left the buttons open, pulled his hat down tight, and scrabbled into his saddle, swinging his heels as he pulled up the tether rope and coiled it by his knee.

He caught up with Mike in a few bounds. 'What do I do?'

'Stick close to me and a little back. For a small favour, our cows are still down. Take a look next time she flashes.'

Cav craned his neck around to where he thought the beef-herd was bedded down. But when the lightning flashed it blinded him. He tried again, keeping his eyes shut, feeling dizzy and as though he was falling from the saddle, but it worked; he opened his eyes on the flash and saw the cows,

60

all down, their long horns outlined against the lightning.

The drumming that he had dreamed was thunder could not be heard now that he was in the saddle. But his horse heard it, or something; he danced, and pawed the ground a little, anxious to work.

Mike said, softly: 'Ahhhh——' and pointed.

An old cow-brute—old from his height and the stretch of his horns—was slowly getting up, front end first, and then the hind end up against the flashing sky. Then another, and another.

'No use talking to 'em,' Mike said. 'Thunder's too loud. I'll head that leader off, and you ride about two horse-lengths behind me and throw in the next one behind him. We'll put them in a long mill, going with the clock, the way they like to go.'

He went off, loping daintily. Cav waited a couple of seconds and followed him. A half-dozen cows were on their feet.

The horse under him was good; fast and lightfooted and aware of what business he was in. He sidled up on a hesitant longhorn, and the steer went off after the one Mike was chowsing.

Cav held in, and waited for another cow and put her in the mill.

Big raindrops began to fall on Cav's wool hat. He buttoned his shirt, and slid deeper in the saddle. The whole herd was up now, but they were moving quietly.

The thunder of the cow-mob from the north was clear now, and steady over the intermittent thunder from the skies.

There was a jingling, and Harry trotted up out of the night, goading the wagon oxen from his saddle. Each team was yoked together, to keep them from running, Cav

E

figured, though they didn't look panicky. Harry took the lead, and Cav trotted up to take over the second yoke.

Mike threw his wild beef in behind them.

The rain kept spattering, not making up its mind to come down good and soaking on them. It wasn't unpleasant, the night was warm, but Cav's wool hat got heavy on his head; the cowmen were wearing expensive felts that shed water like a slicker.

More and more cattle were going into the slow mill, a circle half a mile or more across. Cav forced himself to remember the land as he'd seen it at nightfall. Rocks over that way, must keep the trail herd away from them. A couple of little streams back there, nothing to make cows pile up and hurt themselves, any longhorn could jump them.

'Yonder coming,' Mike yelled, loud but smooth, nothing to panic the animals.

Cav craned and looked. Behind him all of the Grolier Brothers' riders were strung out, edging the mill, making its outside line. Ahead of him Harry goaded a red team of oxen, or was it black? Sometimes they looked one, sometimes the other in the lightning.

There, off to one side, came cows, it seemed like more cows than Cav had ever seen at one time. They were at a dead run, their tongues out, their eyes reflecting the lightning.

Looked like they were going to miss the Grolier herd by a quarter of a mile.

Mike came up and said: 'Spur off an' go help Cav, Li'l Cav. I'll take over your span here.'

Cav nodded, jerked his soggy hat down tighter, and swung his unspurred heels into the K-C horse's flanks. The pony took off with a buck-leap, as though he smelled his

62

own outfit yonder, and then Cav was racing through the night from the milling herd to the racing one.

It occurred to him to wonder what a gopher hole would do to his horse's leg if one showed up. Then he decided he had better not think of things like that. Since he probably couldn't stop his horse if he wanted to—and since stopping might get him run over by the K-C herd—he might as well think happy, cheerful thoughts.

None came.

Thunder rolled, lightning flashed, and a huge cloud of dust rolled at him, turning into mud when it hit his wet face and neck. Seemed like the final insult from sky to man, that it could rain enough to wet you, but not enough to lay the dust. Maybe the galloping K-C cows were biting below the wet ground with their hard hoofs.

A cowboy came up out of the night. He wasn't there one second, was the next, as the lightning flashed. He leaned far out of the saddle of his loping pony and shouted: 'You from Groliers?' The bellow was faint above cow noise and thunder.

'Yeah.'

'Where lies their herd?'

Cav swung his arm in the lightning flash. The rider screamed: 'We better try and point t'other way, then.'

He veered his pony, and Cav fell in alongside him. The rider pulled up, and they stood, their horses blowing. Cowboy said: 'Herd'll be on us, in two, three minutes. Then we take off, ridin' yonder hard as we know. Sometimes cow-brutes'll follow a horse; better if there's two of us.'

'All right.'

'Didn't know Groliers had a boy in their string yonder. You cookie, or what?'

Cav didn't answer that. He wasn't sure he had a job at all.

He'd answered the Groliers mighty pert when they had as good as offered him a job prodding ox; but now, if Big Cav didn't want him, maybe Groliers' feelings would be hurt, and he'd be out on the prairie alone.

The cowboy whooped: 'Yonder coming!' and reached down to haul his cinch tight. As Cav leaned over to do the same thing, the cowboy said: 'Cav was coming up with chuck wagon team, but I guess he didn't make it.' Then he picked up his lines and yelled: 'They call me Yonder,' and took off, riding hard to the right, ahead of the herd.

Cav, riding after him, thought the nickname was no wonder, as that one word seemed to be about half of all Yonder's speaking.

Riding south of this herd was just like riding north of the Grolier cattle; too fast for thinking. If there were any other men with the K-C's than he and Yonder, he couldn't see them; and some of the time he couldn't see Yonder, either; just the rolling hoofs and the rattling horns of the cows, and his own pony's ears and the pommel of his saddle.

Then Yonder pulled up, and walked to Cav to join him, and they stood and let the cows go by. 'Unless I miss my directions and all, yonder's north, and that is just where those cows are heading. We turned 'em, boy. . . . You got a name?'

'Cav Rand.'

Yonder asked what everyone always did, down here in Texas: 'Kin to our boss?'

'No. But I know him.'

They started walking their blown horses north, alongside the cattle. 'Say,' Yonder said, 'that's a K-C pony you're forking.'

'Groliers picked him up straying. They thought I could

64

ride him back to your camp; I'm aiming to ask for a job there.'

'Might get it, if the herd hasn't run over the camp, chuck wagon, bedding and all. . . . They're slowing down yonder.'

It was true. The cattle were still running, some of them, but some were at a trot, and some were dropping out to walk; and even the ones that were running seemed to have lost a little of their pure racehorse ambition. Yonder said: 'Seems like you and I turned a stompede, Cav Rand.'

'My second in a night. I was with Groliers when they got their cows into a mill. But, truthfully saying, theirs didn't stompede. Just acted restless.'

Yonder said: 'This run'll cost Kane and Cavanagh a few tons of tallow. But they'll eat it back; the saying is, the grama grass is rich, up north yonder.' He pulled a short, stubby pipe out of his shirt pocket, and began filling it.

Tired as their horses must be, they were still fast walkers. By the time they came to the K-C camp, marked by a coal-oil lamp on the chuck wagon tongue, the cows were dropping behind them. The sheet lightning storm had stopped, and there wasn't much to see now but the North Star, shining out of a patch of unclouded sky. The rest of the sky was beginning to mackerel up, too, as the storm passed over.

Riders passed between them and the camp lantern, and then they could smell coffee and bacon.

A man rode at them from the north and called: 'That you, Yonder?'

'Me as rode the herd down yonder, and brought it back again.'

Big Cav's deep voice said: 'You might wait for your boss to praise you, instead of heaping it on yourself. I never did catch you; those cream oxen couldn't get my word at all that I wanted them to point the herd.'

'You don't talk ox, mebbe.'

Big Cav's laugh boomed, and the bulk of his horse narrowed and then widened again as he turned to ride into camp with them. 'Who's that on your far side?'

'Grubline rider, brought a stray pony back from Groliers. He made a hand, turning the herd.'

Big Cav said: 'Thanks, then, stranger. The cows don't mean more than all I own in this world. You're welcome to grub with us as long as you feel like it.'

'I was hoping for a job,' Cav said.

Big Cav's saddle creaked. Then he said: 'I've heard that voice before, but it was being worn by a fellow who's back in Louisiana, learning to be something more than a dumb cowpoke.'

66

'Aw, Cav, I couldn't stand that stuffy school, and the weather turning late spring.'

Big Cav's laugh hadn't changed at all. 'Truth is, I've been missing you. Like Yonder says, I don't speak ox-talk; your team pulls all right, but not always in the direction we mean to aim them; not the first time we ask them, anyway.'

'Bo and Billy are used to me.'

Yonder said: 'This the one sold you those oxen, Cav? You let him take over their driving, 'stead of the cook, and old cook'll sing your praises for evermore.'

Big Cav said: 'That's right,' and then they were at the wagon, and the bacon smell was right there, and Cav was hungrier than he had ever been in his life.

The cook was a fat, tired looking man, when Cav could see his face; mostly it was down in the fire-smoke, which didn't seem to bother him at all; his eyes were all scrinched up whether there was smoke in them or not.

Big Cav said his name was Pursely. Cav couldn't figure out if it was a nickname or for real. Big Cav said: 'This fellow helped turn the run back, Pursely. Feed him up good.'

Pursely said: 'Now this outfit's feeding up every empty-belly comes riding along. Man would think a cook had maybe thirty hours in the day, and no need for sleep.'

Yonder said: 'Cook like you needs no time for meals, anyhow, Pursely. Man who knew what you put in those messes of yours would surely not eat them.'

'Go up yonder and drop dead, Yonder.' But while he was talking, Pursely was piling three tin plates high with corn-cake and bacon, beans and wild greens cooked with sow-belly. He poured blackstrap on the corncakes and handed it over.

'Might as well eat it.' He forked two extra strips of bacon on Cav's plate. 'You look skinny to me.'

'Wiry enough to drive oxen,' Big Cav said. He fished the coffee-pot off the iron bars over the fire, and filled his cup.

Pursely said: 'Man doesn't live who could make those ox-beasts do to suit him. They just plain—what you say, boss?'

'Cav here has been goading those oxen since they were calves. It wouldn't hurt him to pick up a goad again.'

'Praise be to the skies,' Pursely said. 'Let the firmaments open and manna pour down! Young fella, want I should kill a fatted calf for you?'

Yonder and Big Cav were laughing, and Cav couldn't help joining in. 'Yonder's one real religious cook,' Yonder said. 'I wouldn'ta suspected the same.'

'Never had nothing to give thanks for, before,' Pursely said. 'Oh, I am glad to be shucked of those white monstrous steers.' He paused. 'Of course, if you expect to work for me, you're gonna have to cut wood and haul water like any other cookie.'

'The birthday party didn't last long,' Big Cav said. 'So be it, then. Throw your saddle in the bed wagon, Cav.'

Cav said: 'Don't I ever get to ride a horse at all?'

Big Cav said: 'You can night ride some. And if Pursely's water and wood is up—not that we'll be in wood country much longer—you can help the night wrangler in the morning. You might as well learn to throw a rope.'

'I've been practising,' Cav said.

'Good, good.' Big Cav wiped out his plate with the last of his corncake, and rinsed it in the boiling dish water, stacked it neatly on the tail of the chuck wagon. He got up, went to the bedding wagon, got his roll. 'Not much night left.' He flipped the bed out on the sandy ground.

Men were riding in from rebedding the cattle, eating and going to sleep or riding out again. Cav got his bed from his grounded saddle, unrolled it near Big Cav's, climbed into it, his boots under his saddle, his hat on the horn.

Big Cav said: 'Bo and Billy'll be glad to see you. . . . Cav?'

'Sir?'

69

Big Cav chuckled. 'First time I've heard that since this outfit formed up. . . . You have aged some in the few weeks since I first saw you. Remember, under that paw-paw tree?'

'Mulberry,' Cav said. The world was whirling around him from his tiredness.

'That's right. . . . I like a boy who has eyes in his head. . . . Cav, are you in any trouble?'

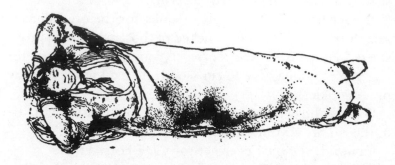

The world stopped whirling as Cav fought his way back to full wakefulness. He would not, could not, lie to Big Cav. But there was Shawnee and Sheriff Smith and, after all, Cav had stolen the grey horse . . . in a way. But he couldn't lie to Big Cav. He scrunched down in his bed, and pressed his cheek to the seat of the saddle.

One of the hands was singing: 'I'm leaving Cheyenne,' to the bedded cattle.

Cav tried to go to sleep, so he wouldn't be making up a lie, pretending to be asleep so he wouldn't have to answer Big Cav's question.

But when he closed his eyes, he saw the horse-thief again, friendless, waterless, a few shreds of socks clinging to his ankles, too tired to pick his way among the cactus thorns.

He would never sleep again, for fear he'd dream he was being turned out for a horse-thief.

70

The Grolier riders thought Big Cav should have hanged the man.

Maybe it would have been kinder.

After a long time, Big Cav grunted, and then turned over in his bed, as though making himself comfortable.

Sleep had left Cav, he thought. But it must have come back sometime, because it was full day when he woke up.

Working for Pursely had its peculiarities. The cook did not follow the road-rider's way of cooking beans; he liked his to cook a long time, and steady. A box of sand rode on the tailgate of the chuck wagon, and one of Cav's duties was to keep a fire going in it, so the beans would cook, slowly and through-and-through all day long.

Since the fire was already going, it was no trouble for Pursely to keep a coffee-pot on, too, and that made him a big man with the riders, who'd drop away from the herd, from riding point—in front,—or swing,—at the side;—or drag—the tail where the big dust was—and come up behind the chuck wagon to have a hot cup, heavy with sugar and canned cow, which was what they called the evaporated milk they whitened their coffee with.

'Cuts the trail dust out of my throat,' Yonder or Pecos, Jim or Ned would say. 'You cook awful, Pursely, but your coffee keeps me from shooting you plumb dead.' Then the rider would grin, and slap his horse's neck with the reins, and race back to his work.

Pursely would laugh at them. 'Trail driver'd sooner shoot himself than ever come out and say he liked the way a man cooks, Little Cav. And I'd sooner give up eating my own cooking than own up to the fact that I think we got a pretty good bunch of riders chowsing this herd.'

The K-C horse he'd ridden in the little stompede was back in the remuda, part of Harry's string; the grey was probably walking with the Grolier cavvy, which was another name for remuda; and no one but Shawnee knew where

Belle was, easy-stepping, fast-moving Belle with the shiny bay coat.

It was hard to walk alongside the oxen with his goad in his hand, or to ride the wagon box alongside Pursely as he drowsed, or to run around behind the wagon to chunk up the fire, all the time calling out to Bo and Billy so they would know he was there.

Hard to walk while the others rode, guarding the cattle, moving easy, or riding up little draws and over the sand-hills to see what the world looked like.

But when Cav felt down in the mouth about his position in life, all he had to do was remember the stuffy house back in Alexandria, and Professor Lovatt's stuffy voice droning away, and the marshmallow tones of the Louisiana boys calling him Alabam' and worse.

Pursely was pleased with him. When Cav was along, Bo and Billy pulled evenly and well, and went where they were supposed to, and didn't bump the wagon wheels over rocks, so that the coffee spilled on the tail-gate fire and put it out. Pursely mostly slept on the box.

The bedding wagon was mule drawn and rough; the night wrangler, who slept in it during the early day, said he purely admired to go join an outfit that had its beds pulled by ox-creatures.

His name was Jerry, and he asked Cav, in all seriousness, if Cav thought they could teach a couple of the beef steers to pull the bed wagon. Cav looked at the long horns and the muscular kicking legs of the herd, and politely declined to try and find out.

That was the way it was on the drive: Pursley the cook, Jerry the night wrangler, Hiram the mule-skinner, and Little Cav the cookie were friends with each other. The riders, the real cowboys who handled the herd, stuck together, doing nothing to make the chore-boys feel lower than the drovers, but just assuming that riders were better than other people.

It was hard to walk in a horseback world.

Mr. Kane was not with them. He had taken his travelling horse and gone ahead to Kansas to set up a market for the cattle. And Cav saw little of Big Cav, after that first night of the little stompede.

Big Cav was the boss, better than the riders, much better than the chore-boys, and he sat by himself when he ate, and nobody put a bedroll within ten feet of him when he slept.

But he didn't do anything to make it that way; it just was.

They kept going north. Once or twice the cattle tried to turn south, once or twice they tried to run instead of walking, but Big Cav knew how to manage a herd, and they didn't get away with it.

Around the fire at night, while the men ate, Cav heard stories of runs, real stompedes that made the little one he'd been in look like a friendly summer shower.

They crossed the Concho, and headed for the Llano River, and when they got there the river was low, and Big Cav called in Yonder and Jim, and they sat around a little fire, and talked and talked.

Cav asked Pursely: 'What's the trouble? That river's just a sand flat, nothing to cross.'

Supper was over, and the coffee-pot was on the campfire, and the oxen were lying in a shallow gully, a draw in cow-talk, munching their corn, turning it over and over between their strong teeth. Work was all done, but Pursely looked as worried as the men by the fire.

'Dry drive,' he said, as though he hated to spare the breath it took to get two words out. 'Dry drive. There are

74

tanks ahead, in the rocks and in the 'dobe, that are some-times full of enough water to pass a herd. If it's been rain-ing. But looky at the old Llano. Been no rain since I don't know when, or the river would be higher.'

Cav looked at the sky. There wasn't a star that wasn't shining bright as brand new; not a one hid its face behind a cloud. Dry night. Dry drive ahead.

Between the camp and the river the cattle lay, bedded down, full of river water and good grama grass, and resting nicely. The night wrangler had the horses down in the river flats; it was a peaceful camp.

For the first time, Cav thought how the men had talked of stompedes and Indian trouble, of prairie fires and light-ning storms, but nobody'd ever told stories about dry driving.

Seemed as though a man who had been through one couldn't bear to remember it.

Yonder and Harry got up and went out towards the cavvy, calling to Jerry for horses. After a while Frank and Pecos rode in from the first watch at night-guarding.

They got their coffee, and Big Cav called them over, and another pow-wow started.

'What do we do?' Cav asked Pursely. 'Go around?'

'There's no go around to this jornada,' Purlsey said. 'It's take it and like it. Nothing to be done. Maybe wait for rain, I dunno. I cook, I don't think.'

Cav asked what a jornada was.

'Day's journey, in Spanish,' Pursely said. 'Not that I talk much of that noble tongue. We use it for any kind of bad trip, from a couple of dry jornadas in New Mexico that have gotten themselves notorious for wiping out a party, now and then.'

Cav went and got his bedroll, unstrapped it, rolled it out.

Then he felt carefully under it for little sticks and stones, and finally, he rolled up his jacket and put it on his boots, and had a pillow.

His saddle he left in the bedding wagon. He felt funny pillowing his head on a saddle he never rode any more.

Big Cav called him out of a deep sleep.

At once he was up, and pulling his boots on. He carried his hat and jacket in his hand, and went on over to where the boss sat by the fire.

Big Cav said, seriously: 'Cav, you're about to see something I wish no man would ever have to see.'

They had come a long way from the mulberry tree in Louisiana. Cav said: 'Yes, sir.'

'Dry drive,' Big Cav said. 'Ninety miles of it. And not a cloud in sight. We can't hold here, on the river; it might not rain for six weeks, now that the spring is over.'

'Yes, sir.'

'We're going to lay over a day or so, get the cattle well watered, full of grass. I'm sending Yonder back to the Groliers to tell them to leave the trail and come up to the river above us, so the herds won't mix. And I'm sending you ahead.'

Cav felt startled. He wanted to say that he didn't want to leave the herd; he wanted to say that he didn't exactly feel like going, alone, into something that frightened people like Big Cav; he wanted to say a lot of things. But he said nothing, and waited for his orders.

'We're going to take the bedding out of the bed wagon, and load her with barrels,' Big Cav said, 'and hitch your team of oxen to her. You'll go ahead and put off a barrel here and there, so's the men can drink, and maybe sponge out the ponies' noses. The cattle'll have to take care of themselves. They'll lose a little tallow, but it can't be

76

helped, and maybe-so, they'll make it back up north a piece. We can let you have six barrels; the others'll go on the chuck wagon. . . . Think you can cut it, boy?'

Cav said: 'Yes, sir.'

Big Cav shook his head. 'You'll have to keep your oxen out of the water, pretty much. They're a good, quiet team, but no man knows what a cow-brute will do when he's crazy thirsty; and, after all, they're cows, or their mothers were. If they'll behave for anybody it will be for you.'

Cav nodded. He felt pretty good.

Big Cav said: 'I don't feel right, sending you alone; but I can't spare a man. After the first dry jornada, the herd's going to want to stompede back here to the river; and that's what the trouble is. It'll take us all and we could use another dozen men. You got any questions, Cav?'

Cav thought a minute. Then he said: 'Why, yes sir. Supposing I run into water? Any way of letting you know?'

Big Cav looked at the clear stars in the sky, he turned his head, as though listening to the dry rustle of the night wind. 'Not a very big chance.'

'But a chance.'

Big Cav nodded. 'What they say: "All signs fail in a drought." You don't have a horse, do you?'

'Big-footed grey, back with the Groliers.'

Big Cav sighed, and looked straight at Cav. He picked up his hands, and made as though he wanted to hold Cav's shoulders. Then he dropped his hands again, and said: 'Yes, I saw him back there. Harry showed him to me. Seemed a pretty funny choice for a man to buy to take out across half of Texas on. You know horses, and you should have had plenty of money left after paying your school bill.'

Cav said nothing.

Big Cav sighed again. 'There's a couple of rules to Texas

living. One of them is that you don't ask a man if his name is the one he was born with, and the other is that you don't ask to see his bill of sale for a horse. Not unless you and he are awfully good friends.'

There was nothing in the world Cav wanted more than to be friends with the big man. But he couldn't say anything. Grey was stolen, no question about it. If he told, Big Cav was sheltering a horse-thief; either that, or Big Cav would have to fire him. And probably worse. Cav wondered if that man had died. . . . Sometimes he could forget the horse-thief for a couple of hours, but not often.

'All right,' Big Cav said. 'The boys have your team out, watering it, making the oxen soak in the river. They can take in a lot through their hides, for all they aren't fixed for sweating. Like you say, you might find water, and you'd want to come back and tell us. We'll tie a horse on your tailgate; that K-C brand you rode up from the Groliers'll do. He purely hates to travel with the cavvy, anyway.'

Cav said: 'Yes, sir,' and turned away.

Big Cav called after him: 'Get some sleep, we'll rout you out after midnight and see you on your way. Tell Pursely I want him.'

Maybe I'll die, out there on the dry drive, Cav thought. Maybe die, and leave Big Cav thinking I was a horse-thief. Well, I am. Paw and Maw would have said that just because a man steals a horse from you, doesn't give you the right to steal one from him. Big Cav would say the same, I reckon. I am a horse-thief.

He lay, lonesome and puzzled, under the clear sky. Hiram was nailing tops on the open barrels, the night guard was singing to the cattle down in the river bottoms, someone was snoring by the fire.

Finally, he fell asleep, and a few minutes later, Pursely was

78

shaking him, and saying: 'Rise and grumble, boy. Time for you to be rolling.'

Cav said: 'All right,' but Pursely stood by till Cav stood up, gave his bed a good shaking, and rolled it nice and tight.

When he took it to the wagon, the men had already loaded the barrels, and were pouring canvas buckets of water into them. Cav stowed his bed under the wagon seat.

Pursely called: 'Come and get it, cookie.'

There was bacon and fresh white bread, toasted, a plate of beans, some wild greens from the river. Pursely said: 'Last good meal you'll see for ninety miles.'

Cav said: 'Three days?'

Pursely said: 'Four, mebbe five. After a day or so, those oxen ain't gonna be so spright as they've been. Eat it up, boy.'

Cav cleaned his plate, and stood up. Jerry was riding up out of the night, and tying the K-C horse to the tailgate of the ox cart. He threw a bridle into the wagon bed and rode away again, back to the night-wrangling.

'I've had worse boys working cookie for me,' Pursely said. 'You sometimes kept the fire going and had water when I needed it. More than I can say of a lot.'

Cav didn't feel like grinning, but the lantern light was on his face, so he made an effort. 'You don't burn the beans every time, Pursely.'

'Take it easy, and it'll come out all right. . . . And whatever you done, there's riders with this very outfit done worse.'

The cook turned away. There it was again.

Cav went and looked over Bo and Billy, made sure their outfits were fitted right. Everything fine. He got his goad from in front of the wagon box, clucked to the oxen, and they put their heavy white shoulders into the yoke and started up. The halter rope came tight on the K-C horse, and he whickered, because he was leaving his friends. But, left alone, he was always drifting away from the cavvy.

Cav gee-hawed the oxen till they were lined out for the ford of the river, and went back to climb over the slowly-moving wheel.

Big Cav came up out of the night then, burly above his saddle, his shape not to be taken for anyone else's against the stars. 'Ride the box till you get across the river. Then get down and walk; don't make your oxen pull a pound more than they have to. . . . Put a barrel of water down about every fifteen miles.'

'How'll I know?'

'First, about every five hours. That'll be sunup. Next, about noon. After that figger it out. . . . If you come to good grass and some shade, maybe mesquite trees or cotton-woods around a dry waterhole, give the oxen their break, and sleep some yourself. . . . But don't let them stompede back to the herd'.

'Bo and Billy'll do to suit me.'

Big Cav said: 'Nobody does to suit anybody on a dry drive. I'll ride the river with you.'

'No need.'

Big Cav's shoulders moved and blotted out a few stars. 'When I am running a herd, no man with it tells me what I have a need to do and no need to do.'

The oxen got to the river, dropped their noses, blew, and then steadily, quietly waded in. The wagon creaked after them, and then went silently, as the water greased the wheels.

Big Cav's horses waded alongside. There was never a time when the long-legged rider had to pull his stirrups up to keep his boots dry; the river was flat down to almost nothing.

They pulled out on the other side, water dripping from the wheels and running down the animals' legs.

Big Cav said: 'There's the North Star. You know to read the sun, daytimes. Don't waste any of the dark, cool time resting; do that in the day. Good luck to you.'

He didn't offer his hand, but raised his reins and swung back for the river.

Cav watched him go.

Then it was too much. He called: 'Cav! Mr. Cavanagh.'

Big Cav rode his pony back. Cav climbed down from the box, took up his goad, went to the oxen's heads, and started the team north. His boss rode alongside, slowly.

Cav said: 'I figure, if a man gets into some trouble, he will be doing his friends no favour by telling them about it.'

'Depends on what kind of trouble,' Big Cav said. You couldn't tell what he was thinking from the tone of his voice.

'Law trouble,' Cav said. 'The way I have heard it, if a man knows that another one has broken the law, and doesn't turn him over to the sheriff, that man is guilty, too.'

'There is not too much law this far west,' Big Cav said. 'A man might not see a sheriff or a Texas Ranger for quite a spell.'

There was no answer to that.

Then Cav said: 'I stole a horse.'

Free of the water, the wagon wheels took up their groaning again; Big Cav's horse jingled his bit, and Bo blew through his nose. The ground was sandy, and gave little heed to the horse's shoes.

Cav looked back to see that the K-C horse was still tied fast to the tailgate.

'What happened to your money?' Big Cav asked. 'You had plenty to mount yourself. Even after paying the school.'

'I still have some. I spent some more on a mare, a real travelling horse.'

'So?'

Cav said, all in a rush: 'A man lawed her from me. He swore to a paper, and a sheriff put me in jail and gave this man my horse. So I stole another horse from him, and came on to the trail.'

Big Cav seemed to be considering this, riding slow alongside the wagon. He said, finally: 'I wish Jeff Kane was here. I'm far from learned in the law. You stole a horse, you are sure of that?'

'The big-footed grey I rode to the Groliers on.'

'This man will be looking for you?'

'I don't know. He has papers to show that Belle is his. The travelling mare I bought in Alexandria. I had papers, too, but the sheriff took them away; this Shawnee said I had forged 'em. That right, forged?'

Big Cav's voice was heavy. 'That's the right word, Cav. Must have been a dumb kind of sheriff. I can see a kid like you stealing a horse, if he had to—well, maybe I can. But I can't see you filling out papers to fool the law.'

A great load fell off Cav's shoulders. He felt like crying. Instead, he waved the goad at Bo, and said: 'Gee, gee,' and then, 'Haw', to get the team going straight again.

Because he felt bad about correcting Bo and Billy when they hadn't done anything wrong, he stepped in as though to fuss with their harness, and gave each of them a rub on the nose.

'Shawnee?' Big Cav asked. 'That's his name?'

'I don't know his real one. He gave the sheriff one, something-or-other Davis.'

'We got a herd of cattle on our hands,' Big Cav said. 'When we're shuck of them, we might be paying this Shawnee a call. You and me and maybe Yonder. Yeah, and Pursely'd like to make a hand. He seems to fancy the way you garner wood.'

Cav said: 'I didn't want to tell you. Make me look an awful kid, letting a peddler and a country sheriff do me that way.'

Big Cav began to laugh. 'I never said you were much for bright, but you're fine for stout,' he said. 'You get your work done. And you know a mulberry from a paw-paw.'

He laughed again, and picked up his reins. His pony, fresh from the river and the river bottom grass, danced. 'Take it easy, Cav. We'll come along as fast as we can.'

'So long—Big Cav.'

It seemed to Cav that Big Cav grinned, in the starlight, and then the pony had whirled, and was single-footing back to the river and the herd and their work, which was loading the cattle with water before the dry drive.

Cav swung the goad as he went along, like a fancy-dressed band major leading the drums and fifes on the Fourth of July.

9

THAT first night was nothing; Cav swung along beside his team as though he was strolling by a creek back in Alabama. The oxen, their stomachs filled with good, green food, walked quietly, the wagon and its barrels of water no strain on the yoke. The stars swung overhead, telling the time.

After false dawn, it got cold, and when he licked his lips, there was a little taste of salt there, as though he'd been sweating earlier, and the sweat had run down and dried.

It seemed a long time from that first grey light until the sun was really up and biting into the chill. Then he was hot, just the beginnings of it, and he stopped the team and took two planks from the bed of the wagon and rolled a keg down it. He looked around to make sure there was nothing to hide the water barrel from the K-C riders.

Well, not much. Cactus, and rocks, some mesquite. He took his knife and cut arrows in the mesquite bark, pointing at the water keg; he took a stone and broke some prickly pear cactus over the bend towards it.

He had drunk no water since the river, nor had his animals. He swallowed a little, now, and took the rags Pursely had given him and sponged out the noses and mouths of Bo and Billy and the K-C horse.

Then he decided to walk awhile before he grazed them.

It was maybe not the best decision in the world. The walking was warm, not hot, which was good; but by nine o'clock—or what he guessed was nine o'clock—the grama-covered loam gave way to a surface of hard rock. Maybe

84

granite, maybe lava, maybe the malapie he'd heard the men talk of, but had never seen; at any rate it didn't seem to grow anything but little clumps of verbena or hill-of-gold, both of them brown now in the drought.

Bo and Billy dropped their heads a little and began swinging their noses from side to side as though they were mad. They had been family pets a long time, and they had come from a wet country, along the Black Warrior River and through Louisiana and East Texas.

They were facing something they had not seen before. Well, so was Cav.

Their ox shoes rang on the rock.

The K-C horse seemed to have enough of all this. Looking back, Cav saw him on his hind legs. First he would try and break the halter that held him to the wagon; then he would try and climb aboard. Probably smelled the water that kept the barrel staves tight by seeping out.

Cav went back and shortened the halter, pulling it through the wagon post like he was snubbing a bull down. Then he sponged out the horse's nose and mouth again. The K-C horse snapped at the sponge.

But Bo and Billy, mad or not, were good old boys. They slugged away over the lava at a steady walk, heads down, tongues out.

Finally the rock gave way to a patch of sand. Nothing grew here, but it was at least soft to the feet. Cav halted his little train, and treated himself to a swallow of water from his saddle canteen, which was under the wagon seat.

Sun was fair up by now, and he was losing weight. He could tell it by his belt, which he had tightened to the last hole. He got his pocket knife and made another hole, and gee-upped the team.

In this dry air, you didn't know you were sweating; it

popped out and dried before a man was aware of it. But he could feel salt caking on his cheekbones and in his eyebrows, and when he took his hat off, his hair was soaking. He ran his fingers through it, and trudged on.

Towards high noon a clump of mesquite trees came out of the north and he walked them down, and halted again.

He unyoked Bo and Billy with care, and tied each of them to a tree. They could eat all the mesquite beans they wanted, for what good it would do them. He took the K-C horse to another tree, and tied him up good, though, as a rule, horses do not have the fondness for mesquite that cows do. Still even a mesquite was a tree, of sorts, and might give a little shade.

Cav got plenty of that for himself, by crawling under the wagon bed. He was arguing with himself like a pair of country lawyers whether to eat first or sleep first when he must have gone off.

So far as he knew, he didn't dream at all. He just woke up after a while with so little idea of where he was that he cracked his head on the under side of the wagon bed.

But it didn't do much harm, because he'd gone to sleep with his hat on.

His eyes were salt caked and glary, and his tongue felt big as Bo's or Billy's. Climbing out from under the wagon, he looked at his stock first; all three of them still tied fast, and standing droopy-headed.

He filled a washbasin with water and let them drink, first Bo, then Billy, then the K-C horse. The horse fought his rope like he was crazy-mad when he smelled the water going to the oxen, but he was tied overhead, and the limber mesquite went with his dancings and gave him no help in breaking his tie-rope.

Another swallow from the canteen brought Cav's tongue

86

down to fit, and he spanned in and took up the goad, and the wagon went forward.

The mesquites lasted about an hour. On their north edge he skidded another barrel down for the riders when they came, and goaded on.

About an hour before sundown a little breeze came up. It was not a very cool breeze, but it seemed to help a little, and the team carried their heads a little higher.

Then it was dark, and he got some corncake and cold, crisp bacon out of the wagon and chewed it as he walked along. It hadn't seemed possible to get up an appetite, dry as he was, but the food didn't taste bad. The salt in the bacon was particularly good, which was funny; he'd have thought that a dry man would hate salt.

He remembered what some of the riders had said, around the fire, about horses in desert country going for the salt cakes before they would drink, and thought that maybe man was more like the beasts than the preachers admitted.

At midnight, when he went to skid down the third barrel of water, he found he hardly had the strength for the job.

He took a break, punching another hole in his belt before he lost his pants, and drinking a little water on top of another strip of bacon, and the barrel was down on a high rock, where the drovers would surely see it.

Billy bawled like a bull at leaving the barrel behind, and the K-C horse nickered and whinnied.

There was starlight aplenty to see by, and he hardly ever stumbled over a rock, or put his foot into a critter's hole-house. He got to thinking that, though there were plenty of burrows around, he had not seen a prairie dog or a gopher since he didn't know when. Maybe there was water down deep in their underground villages or maybe they just slept down there and waited for the rain to wake them up.

He got to wondering how it would be to be a gopher, safe in a hole in the ground with no worries about going any place, or taking any cows along with you. Pretty good.

Maybe he was going crazy.

It was a funny thing that he didn't really feel thirsty; his throat and mouth weren't too dry, he was just so tired that it didn't seem possible he could keep walking. But he

could lift a foot, and make it fall ahead of him and then lift the other, and somehow keep going.

Ahead there was something coming, and he stopped and looked at it, and then the oxen stopped, too.

It was the dawn, it was the light coming up. So he swung to the east, he figured, after a while. He swung the goad, and shouted: 'Gee,' at Bo and Billy.

They just stood there.

Stumbling, he got out the dishpan, and filled it. He was so weak he could not raise it in his hands, once it was filled; so he took some of the water for himself, waited a few minutes, and managed to get the pan in front of Bo and Billy without spilling a drop.

Tired and sick as they were, the oxen were trained. Billy waited till Bo had drunk and been goaded away, and then he drank.

Then they gee'd, and Cav found he wasn't so far off the trail at that. The K-C horse was dancing with rage because everybody had drunk but him. When Cav sponged him out, he snapped at the rag.

Two hours after sun-up, they came to some cottonwoods, a sure sign of water. But the hole was dry, and when Cav tried to dig down, he hit rock almost at once, and had to give up; the rocks were sticky with dry, brown moss.

He tied each of the animals to a cottonwood and got under the wagon for a sleep.

When he woke up, the oxen and the K-C horse had all gnawed the bark off the trees he had tied them to. He gave Bo and Billy some corn, and even fed a couple of long ears to the horse, and then ate corncake and sucked bacon. His mouth felt strange and sore and sort of swollen, and it was hard to chew.

He left a barrel of water under the cottonwood trees. Even if he was off the trail—and he didn't think he was— any rider would investigate under those trees.

When night came, he reckoned he had covered more than half of the dry jornada. Maybe two-thirds. But the oxen were stumbling and sick, and he had hit no water that would permit him to get on the K-C and ride back, a big man bringing news to the herd.

Now he knew that Big Cav had never expected him to find water. But the K-C horse was a wanderer and a nuisance to Jerry on the night wrangle, and if it made Cav feel more hopeful to have him along, it was all right with Big Cav.

That night was never clear to Cav, afterwards. It was a night of walking and falling, of goading the oxen and sometimes giving them a little water to make them keep going, of finding himself hanging on to the wagon for help, and having to make his hands let go, so as not to burden the already playing-out Bo and Billy.

He must have done right, because in the morning he saw there was only one barrel left, and that was the one they had been using. He must have put down a barrel sometime.

He climbed into the wagon, and thumped it. More than three-quarters full.

When he put it down, he was free to walk ahead to water; he could even cut the horse loose and let him find his own way, or he could get on the horse. Yes, that was it. When he put that last barrel down, he could climb into his saddle on the K-C and leave Bo and Billy to bring the wagon along by themselves.

If Big Cav lost his team and wagon that way, it was his own fault. Shouldn't have sent a single man on this dry jornada. Should have—

He slept from maybe mid-morning till mid-afternoon— evening, the Texas riders called it—and then sponged down the stock and tried to drive.

Bo and Billy had gone blind.

It was too much. In Texas or any place else, it was too much.

He didn't even have a gun with him, to shoot them with, when they had dropped the last barrel. Just a little, short-bladed pocket knife. Doubted if it would cut through ox-hide.

He gee-upped, and they went ahead. But now they wouldn't go if he didn't talk to them, and talking hurt his throat, made him feel like blood was running down the inside of it.

He told them about Mary and her little lamb, he told them about the Chisum Trail, talking because he couldn't sing more than a croak, he told them about Hickory, Dickory, Dock. He tried to tell them about The Old Rugged Cross, which had been his mother's favourite hymn, but halfway through he forgot the words and had to go back to the school-going lamb and the mouse-running clock.

The blind oxen followed his voice, and he staggered

91

along ahead of them. There was a new moon tonight, or he thought there was; anyway it seemed lighter than it had the other two nights of the dry jornada. Wasn't anything wrong with his eyes, and there didn't seem to be anything wrong with the horse's either.

Every so often Bo and Billy would stop, for all of his talking, and just stand with their heads down. Then they'd pick up and go ahead a little.

Even if he found water now, it was too far to ride back to the herd to tell them. So he brought the K-C horse around to the front of the team, and tied his rope around the pole and to the horn, and tried to make the horse pull.

The horse went straight up on his hind legs, nearly ditching Cav, but he managed to stay in the saddle and get the rope tight.

But when he did this, Bo and Billy stopped. They weren't going to walk unless he did. So he got down again, and started to take the K-C horse's bridle off and re-tie the halter to the tailgate.

Then he thought, why go to all that trouble? He'd turn the horse loose. Maybe it would save the animal's life.

Cav was so beat-up in the head by then he almost took the halter off while his good saddle was still on the horse's back. He brought himself around in time, and undid the cinch and slipped the saddle. Then he finally took the halter off, and the K-C went off a few feet and rolled; he'd been saddled longer than is good for horsehide.

Now Cav found that he wasn't man enough to heave his own saddle into a wagon bed. And he had planned to be a cowboy!

A drink of water, a mighty small one, did for that, and a bite of cornpone. The bacon had gone bad on him, it smelled of mildew and he couldn't swallow it. He drank and ate just enough to give him saddle-lifting strength, and went back to the oxen.

All his fiddling around with horses and saddles and corn-pone and water had given the team a little time for resting, and they walked off at a good clip, maybe a full mile an hour.

The horse followed the wagon almost as close as if the tie rope still ran to his head. Cav had halfway thought he would turn back towards the herd, and maybe die of thirst on the way, but he seemed to have made a family of Cav and the oxen. Or maybe it was the water barrel on the wagon his nose was following.

After a while the moon set, and for some reason, Cav decided that this was the time to set off the last barrel. He filled his canteen first, and gave each of the oxen a pan of water. He gave one to the horse, too; he had to, to keep him away from Bo and Billy while they drank, and even so, Cav had to stand there chunking rocks at the K-C.

When he got the barrel down, it was a problem how to leave it so the K-C horse didn't kick it over. So he spent another quarter pan tolling the horse in and putting his halter back on and tying him off to the tailgate again. He left the saddle in the wagon bed; a little more work for the oxen, but less for Cav.

Those were fine oxen, a great team. A little rest, a little water, and they were ready to go again. It almost seemed like Billy could see Cav's hand when it was passed in front of his eyes.

They walked on north.

Now it didn't matter to anybody but Cav how the last canteen of water was spent, and he mopped out the ox-mouths and noses pretty often, even used the wet rag to wipe their eyes, which maybe didn't help them any except to make them feel good.

He was careful never to take his hat off now; the water in his hair was worth too much to lose.

Sometime that night a wind came into their faces, from directly under the North Star, and they all walked better, and Cav stopped thinking thoughts about letting the wagon go and walking out of there with Bo and Billy. They could make it quite a lot farther without a wagon tied to their yoke.

If he left the wagon, maybe the drovers could bring it along; but the horses would be in bad shape, and maybe not used to pulling, and certainly none of the herd cattle could get into the yoke.

Big Cav had paid him for the wagon, he was entitled to keep it.

Dawn came up flaming red. Sometimes that meant moisture in the sky and sometimes it meant dust. Whichever this one meant, there wasn't much any of them—Cav, the oxen, or the horse—could do about it.

Except keep on walking.

Well, it might pay to dodge the noon heat by sleeping under the wagon. But even in the shade it was hot, and he would lose some more water, and the canteen wasn't too heavy now.

So they all walked on.

It was afternoon, at least the sun seemed to be westering a little, when the K-C horse broke his bridle, and went off across the prairie, kicking up his heels and whinnying.

Cav watched him go without tears. Not that he had water in his eyes to cry with; but he muttered something about good riddance, and he and Bo and Billy walked along, the blind oxen with their noses nearly on the ground.

When they stopped, he would give them a wash out, and

himself a swallow, and that would just about end the canteen. It——

All of a sudden, Cav Rand, who had never thought he'd smile again, was grinning like a fool at a watermelon picnic.

K-C horse had run away; right. K-C horse was almost worn down to a nub; right. Horse that's that far gone doesn't get the strength to break his halter except if something moves him, and strong; right.

Could be, of course, that there was a snake in the wagon bed under the K-C's nose. Could be, but it didn't seem likely.

No, the way that pony had gone galloping north, meant only one thing.

He had smelled water.

Cav croaked: 'Gee-up, boys,' at Bo and Billy, and it seemed to him that they were, if not exactly trotting, at least not staggering quite as much as they had.

When they got to the Colorado, there was the K-C horse, lying down in it. Cav let the oxen drink, while he lay beside them and soaked his head. After they were yoked-out and in the river, he got in himself, clothes and all.

It sure felt wonderful.

IO

By the time the herd was a cloud of dust on the southern sky, Bo and Billy could see again. It was a load off Cav's mind, and a thing to puzzle about; men didn't go blind from thirst, nor horses; why should cattle?

The two oxen and the horse were grazing quietly along the bank, where the ground went easy into the water. It was a good ford; Cav had walked it, ridden it, driven the cattle over it.

Now he went and saddled the K-C horse and filled his canteen, and rode towards the cloud of dust. He maybe should take the oxen with him, in case the herd wanted to make a cow-killing run for the water, but it would slow him down; and anyway he doubted if the sight and smell of two well watered oxen was going to slow the beef down after that dry jornada.

Bo and Billy raised their heads to watch him go, and then went back to filling out their flanks with good river grass.

The horse was sunken in at the flanks, too, but coming back. His coat even had a little shine to it; when he had first come out of the river, the water had run off him in a funny way, because all his hair oil had been burned off on the dry drive.

This was something Cav had learned, too. Cattle went blind and horses lost their hair oil from too much sun and too little water.

Nobody had told him about that. In fact, men around a drive camp fire didn't talk about dry drives at all; just about

96

little, simple things like stompedes and floods, rustlers and Indian attacks.

The K-C had a rough gait when you put him to the lope. Cav rested both hands on the big Mexican pommel and stood up in the stirrups and let the horse trot, not a good cow-pony gait, but one that covered the miles.

Less than an hour from the river he came on Yonder, riding point.

The cows behind him were swinging worse than Bo and Billy had, for all they had not had to pull a heavy wagon up the jornada.

Cav didn't ask how Yonder was, or any pink tea nonsense like that. He just untied the canteen and handed it over.

Yonder rolled water in his mouth a long time, swallowed it, and said: 'George is riding swing, yonder.'

Cav took the canteen back, and made to go. But Yonder asked: 'How far to the river?' He gulped and added, 'Yonder?'

'No more than five miles,' Cav said.

'We might make it,' Yonder tried to smile, but it failed.

Cav rode around the herd, handing out the canteen to each rider as he came to him. Most of the men grunted a quiet, one-word thanks; they were as beat-up a bunch of cowboys as Cav had ever dreamed of.

He came to Big Cav last, riding swing up near the point. Big Cav took the canteen, and as the other men had, took a small sip and rolled it around in his mouth.

Cav said: 'Drink up. The others have had theirs.'

'I'm out of the habit,' Big Cav said. He smiled, not much more successfully than Yonder had done. Then he took another sip, and handed the canteen back. 'Have any trouble?'

'Easy as putting out the cat on a warm evening.'

'I'll bet.' Big Cav stood in the saddle and rolled a little to ease his legs. The water he had drunk was already cutting the croak out of his throat. 'We found all of your barrels. Looked mighty favourable to us.'

'It's about five miles to the river. Any chance the cattle stompeding?'

'Oh, they will, they will,' Big Cav said. 'Most of the boys were in one army or another back in the War. Ride around and tell them to throw the cows in a line of skirmishers.'

Even Cav knew what that was, though he had only been four years old when the War ended—it meant to scatter out, and all go ahead side by side. He rode around and told the men, and Yonder and Big Cav held the point till the drag and swing men could bring the laggard cattle up. When they were spread across the prairie no more than two or three cows deep at any point, Big Cav swung his hat, and they rode back through the cows and started them forward, all men now riding drag.

More than half the herd had gone blind. It was a terrible sight, but no great worry to Cav, now that he had seen Bo and Billy get their sight back by lying in the river.

He held the jog-trotter of a K-C horse down to match the pace of the gaunted-down cows and men and ponies. Big Cav sidled his horse over to him.

'Jerry and Pecos are holding the horse-cavvy back and to the west. Ride and tell them to go around the cows and let the horses run for the river; they won't drown each other like cows would.'

'Yes, sir.'

Big Cav said: 'My name'll do, partner,' and grinned his tired grin. 'We don't use many 'sirs' in the cow-droving business, Cav.'

'All right, Big Cav.'

'You'll prob'ly pass Pursely on the way. Tell him to make it to water any way he can; the mules are better off than any of us.'

Cav cut the wheel-tracks of Pursely's trail back about a mile from the last cow. He had to ride forward to find the cook-wagon. It was piled high with the lashed-on empty barrels Cav had left along the dry jornada. Hiram was driving mules, Pursely was nodding on the wagon seat.

Cav rode alongside and prodded the cook, and said: 'Jump off and swim, Pursely.'

Pursely woke up and blinked. The nice, round paunch— a purse, in Texas talk—that had given him his name was largely gone. 'Hi, Cav,' he said. 'Sorry, there's no coffee on the tailgate today.'

'How could there be, without me to keep the fire up? . . . River's less than five miles from the front of the herd. Cav says get there any old way you can.'

Pursely said: 'Now you are going to see some mule driving as is mule driving,' and reached out and took the reins from Hiram's hands. Hiram never said a word.

Pursely slapped the line down on the mule backs and let out what he meant to be a whoop. But it came out somewhere between a croak and a groan. Still, together with the slapping reins, it got the mules up into a walk that was a degree faster than the shuffle they had been going at.

As they rode away, Cav looked the mules over critically. They—just maybe—had come through the dry drive a little better than Bo and Billy had. But they had had more use of the water barrels, for sure, and they were pulling the lighter load; nothing weighed so heavy as water.

He shrugged, and rode on out to tell Pecos and Jerry, the day and night horse wranglers, to let the cavvy run for the river.

II

THEY lay along the river for two days getting the cattle back into shape. Cav and Big Cav rode north a piece, seeing how the going was, and it was not bad; springs that Big Cav remembered from other drives were still running, maybe not so strong as in good years, but plenty good enough.

Big Cav said, as they nooned by one of the streams that gushed out of a cleft rock: 'I haven't told the boys about your trouble with that peddler, what's his name.'

'Shawnee, he called himself,' Cav said. 'Thanks, Big Cav. I guess I acted like a pure fool.'

'Don't see what else you could have done,' Big Cav said. 'And you a boy alone. Take some blame myself, talking you into that sugarmouth school. Jeff Kane ran away from it; why not you?'

'Still——'

Big Cav waved a hand at him. 'No use telling the boys. They see you are all right with me, you'll be all right with them. They had begun worrying about that big-footed grey horse. Nothing pardons a man to steal someone else's horse.'

'I did steal Grey.'

Big Cav shrugged. 'You didn't leave the peddler afoot. You left him a horse worth two of the kind the grey is. Your mare Belle. So forget it.'

They turned south again, and rode an easy clip back to the herd. When they came over the last ridge, a buggy was standing in the river with the chuck wagon and the bed wagon, which had been pushed in to tighten their wheels after the dry drive.

'Hey,' Big Cav said, 'there's Jeff Kane.'

Mr. Kane was sitting on a driftwood log near where Pursely had set up his chuck box and fire. 'Cav, it's good to see you. Li'l Cav, how does it go?'

'Fine, Mr. Kane.'

Pursely said: 'It won't go so fine, if you don't scamper down to the river and get me some firewood. Jerry's been doing for me, and he ain't no flash.'

Cav laughed, and went down to the flats along the river, where every cove had its pile of driftwood. The river was low, and the wood was dry and shining white in the hot sun.

When he got back, he heard Mr. Kane telling Big Cav that their cattle were sold. 'All we got to do is drive to Abilene, Kansas. We'll make us some money this year.'

Cav was looking at the buggy, and then over at the cavvy, where a couple of strange horses must be the ones that had hauled Mr. Kane to them. They looked fat and sleek. 'Mr. Kane, you didn't cross the dry jornada?'

Mr. Kane laughed. 'No, sir. I leave such things to my partner here. I came around through the east, where the farming country lies. Out of the way, but more comfortable.'

Big Cav said: 'But you can't drive cattle that way. Too many fences, too many ploughmen. Coming west again, did you run into the Groliers?'

Mr. Kane began to laugh. 'Yes, sir. They hit the river yesterday about ten miles east of here. They had a mighty hard dry drive. Lost a few head.'

Big Cav sounded angry. 'Not like you to laugh at a friend's trouble, Jeff.'

Mr. Kane said: 'Sorry.' But he was still laughing. 'That is not the joke, of course. They are one mad bunch of cowboys, Cav. While they were waiting down on the Llano to water up their stock, they got took in a horse race. Not a man in the outfit didn't lose a month's pay, and Harry and Mike—why this summer isn't going to pay them at all. They have lost their profit in advance.'

The riders were drifting into the fire. Yonder said: 'Tell, Mr. Kane.'

Mr. Kane reached out and filled his tin cup. 'It goes like this. There they were, strung along the Llano, building up their cows and minding their own business, when this peddler shows up.'

Big Cav looked at Cav. Cav was listening; but after all, the world was full of peddlers.

'Easy spoken man, the way they tell it,' Mr. Kane said. 'Just rode into camp, asking if any cowboy needed needle, thread, a new neckcloth, that sort of thing. Well, what trail drover doesn't? He made a good thing out of the Grolier boys, and just to show his appreciation, peddler gave each customer a brand new German silver belt buckle. So they asked him to spend the night with them, couldn't do less.'

The wind blew overhead, the coffee cups clinked on the mouth of the pot, on the rocks, thudded on driftwood logs pulled up for chairs and tables. Cav listened. Mr. Kane chuckled again. 'Peddler was riding an old buggy with a bay mare and a spavined old mule pulling him. Around the campfire that night, he got to bragging, said his mare was the greatest in the West. Slow and easy in the harness, never out-walked the mule at all, but put a racing saddle on her, and she was faster than a north wind in Amarillo. Could outrun anything this side of Kentucky, and he wasn't too sure of those Kentucky thoroughbreds keeping up with her.

'Well, you know Mike and Harry Grolier. Louisiana boys, they'll bet on anything. Wouldn't be surprised if their granddaddy dealt cards on the river. . . . They play it easy enough, though, bet maybe a ten spot that Mike's sorrel can outrun the peddler's mare. Peddler takes them up on it, and goes off to his bedroll; they'll run in the morning.'

Big Cav said: 'That horse of Mike's can truly travel.'

Mr. Kane chuckled. 'So the Groliers opined. The boys, now, the riders, they held off betting, being working men with a long winter ahead. . . . Lot of good it did them. There's the peddler, snoring away in his blankets; there's his bay mare, eating night grass with the rest of the cavvy. You just know what they did.'

'Took her out for a little moonlit pasear,' Pursely said. 'A little stroll, sort of.'

Mr. Kane said that Pursely was mighty right. 'And, boys —I am merely repeating the words of Mike Grolier, also of his brother Harry, also of every man in the outfit including the cookie—that bay mare could not run, could not trot, she could just about outwalk a tired milk cow.'

Mr. Kane began laughing: 'I had to lend the Grolier fellows money to buy chuck when they come to a town. . . . Stripped, every one of them. Because, it seemed that mare was no night runner, but she was a dawn thunderbolt, she was a locomotive engine on the Santa Fé Railway, she was maybe half antelope and the other half New Mexico road-runner. The race was over about the time Mike and his sorrel left the post; the bay mare was over the finish line and eating grass.'

The drovers roared. But Big Cav was looking thought-ful. 'This peddler got a name?'

Mr. Kane shrugged. 'Man with all that Grolier money doesn't need a name. I think Harry said he called himself McShawn, or thereabouts. . . . So he says thank you, and rides off to the east with all the Grolier money.'

Cav looked at Big Cav, who looked back at him and slowly nodded. Belle had looked just like her stiff-legged, slow-moving sister. Just exactly alike.

Big Cav said, easy as could be. 'This fella went east?'

Mr. Kane said: 'He was about out of stock. And anyway, who'd drive a buggy up the dry jornada?'

12

NORTH again, under the summer sun, the grass showing a little brown from drought, the creeks running a little low, but both grass and water good enough for the herd. One cow died from the dry drive, and another remained blind, but made out all right, apparently from listening to where the other animals went and how they did with their hoofs.

Cav drove Bo and Billy, and fetched wood for Pursely and saw that the water barrels were full, and sometimes when the work was all done in the evening, he put his saddle on the K-C horse and rode out a little, or helped Jerry with the night wrangling, or the hands with the night herding.

Three days north of the end of the dry drive, the prairie sky began to cloud up; first with big white thunderheads, fluffs of cotton in the sky, and then with black clouds, that blacked out the sun and robbed the herd of their shadows.

One by one the riders went into the bed wagon and got their slickers and tied them down behind their saddles.

Pursely said: 'Got you a turnwater coat, Cav?'

Cav shook his head.

'There's some extra tar-pole-eons in the bedding wagon. Better cut you a poncho and a spare square for headgear.'

The bedding wagon was ahead. Cav handed his goad to Pursely, and started trotting ahead. Yonder, riding in from the herd, saw him and came alongside; Cav hung on to his stirrup, and made the trip at a nice lope.

Hiram had a poncho on already. Cav saw what it was, just an oblong of canvas with a slit for the neck, and pawed over the extra ground sheets in the wagon bed till he found one to his suiting. He dropped off the wagon.

Back of him, Yonder was standing by his horse, making the yellow slicker fast to the cantle. He called: 'Cut a strip off the bottom for your headpiece. Wear the short side in front. . . . Yonder comes a lulu, and that's a fact.'

Cav looked in the direction of Yonder's pointing arm. South-west, sort of. The clouds there filled the sky, and came down and blocked off the prairie, too. As he watched, fine black lines started streaking across the clouds he had thought were so black that nothing darker could be written on them.

'Cloudburst,' Yonder said. 'Oh, how we would have liked this, yonder on that dry drive.'

'Think they're getting it back there?'

'Don't know. Paid to push those cows yonder, not to think. Anything could be so, though. It's a mighty sudden country.' Yonder stepped into the saddle, raised a hand. 'Let's lay out to do. Cows ain't gonna relish this.'

Cav trotted back to the chuck wagon. Pursely was already slickered up. He said: 'Might as well put that on now as any other time. For a while it looked like she might go around us, but she didn't choose to.'

Cav slid the poncho over his head, twisted the extra strip around his wool hat. There was a strong ground wind blowing now; Pursely had to shout to tell him to go dump the cooking fire on the tailgate, and button up the wagon, as he put it.

When the glowing coals hit the ground they went away fast, straight out. Big Cav would have bawled him out good for that ordinarily—well, so would Pursely—for fear of a prairie fire; but the first drops of the rain were already spattering around him. He put the empty firebox in the body of the wagon, threw up the tailgate and dropped the pins home to hold it, and started lacing the canvas.

The white cloth fought him in the rising wind. He could hang onto the canvas, but he couldn't get a hand loose to start the lacing. Then the wind switched around to the north for a minute, and he got the first two eyelets together, and worked fast; before the heavy gusts came on him again, the lacing was over his head, and the canvas was licked.

The rain stung like pebbles. Cav ran around to the team, and took the goad from Pursely, who ducked down to protect his face and stumbled to the off wheel and up into the wagon seat. Cav put one hand on the yoke to steady himself as the gusty wind tried to make a sailboat out of him and his poncho.

Big Cav rode up and yelled: 'We're going to let the herd drift ahead of the storm. Just follow along.' Then he rode off again, and was out of sight fifty feet from the oxen's noses.

The world went under water then, water that marched up the prairie in thick green walls, water that found every crack in a fellow's neck and sent cold streams crawling down his back, water that got in your ears and your nose and into your mouth, too, when you tried to use that for breathing.

Bo and Billy, with the wagon between their tails and the storm, marched on, slower and slower as the firm prairie turned to gumbo and the wheels of the wagon began picking up spongy chunks of it, and dropping them to be run over by the rocking, groaning wagon.

They were alone in the world, he and the oxen. Pursely had crawled into the wagon body, or maybe he had fallen off and swum away.

Water boiled over Cav's boots and up into the tops of them. Each step he took he thought he'd lose one of the boots in the mud; it was gummy enough to pull the nails out of the ox-shoes.

He plodded on.

There was something so mean about being in a flood a few miles north of that terrible dry jornada that you sort of wanted to lie down and cry, if only there was a dry place to lie down on.

Meanwhile he might as well walk alongside his ox-team, long as they would walk. He didn't think that would be much longer.

But it was Cav who stopped first. A boot came halfway off, trapped in the gumbo. He had to bend down and grab hold of its slippery top with both hands to pull it loose.

When he did that, the water-sodden wind got a good, fair chance at him. It knocked off his hat and his tarpaulin head cover and sent them floating northwards. It drove sheets, buckets it seemed, of water between his neck and his collar and drenched his whole body.

Then it picked up his poncho, filled it with air and water and pounded it till it knocked Cav down and rolled him over in the six inches of water that covered the ground. He managed to stagger to his feet only after he had slid the poncho over his head and bundled it up to his chest.

He stood up, staggering and covered with mud. But the mud didn't stay with him—the rain knocked it off again. He turned each side of him to the storm, and it was like a volunteer fire department was giving him its three-alarm treatment.

He was alongside the wagon. By holding to the little knobs over which the top was laced, he managed to get even with the box. Bo and Billy had stopped. He grabbed Billy's tail and the ox was too storm-beat to show his resentment with a cow-kick; he just stood there and let Cav pull himself forward. Clinging to the yoke with one hand, he fumbled at the harness with the other; he had some idea of unyoking and tying the oxen to the yoke, loosely, so they could turn and try and avoid the worst of the storm.

But he couldn't stand up without holding on, and he couldn't unbuckle wet leather with one hand.

So he crept back to the wagon and tumbled up on the box and into the body.

Pursely, huddled in one corner, said: 'Went fishin' and fell in, huh?'

Cav's teeth were chattering. He couldn't remember ever being warm, not to mention so hot and dry he had thought he was going to go under. Just couldn't remember last week, or even yesterday.

Pursely said: 'Shuck out of them wet clothes. Don't you know you're a human bean, an' not a fish nor a polliwog? I got some clean flour sacks here some place or other. Here . . . rub yourself down, and you might live. Got some cough medicine I made.' Trail cooks were supposed to be doctors, of sorts.

Rubbing himself with the flour sacks that Pursely washed out and kept for dish towels, Cav said: 'I don't need any medicine. Not of yours, anyhow. I know what you put in those bottles.'

'That's gratitude,' Pursely said.

109

The dry towels chafed some warmth back into Cav's body; the tarp that Pursely gave him kept it in. He began to feel human again; he even ate a cold pone and a tin dish of beans that were, to his amazement, still warm from the fire they had pitched out of the tailgate. It had all happened faster than beans could cool!

Pursely was muttering that he hadn't signed on to be a sailor. Cav went to sleep. . . .

When he woke up, sun was shining through the canvas, and Pursely was gone. He climbed out of the wagon, and stood by Bo and Billy, who were still steaming from the rain. He guessed the coming of the sun had waked him up. . . .

Holding the tarp around him, he looked around. There was Pursely, on the other side of the oxen, looking forlorn.

All around them, water ran in rivulets and brooks on the low folds of the prairie. On the ridges the grama grass and the wild barley were beginning to stand up again. As each stalk got upright, it snapped away a few shining beads of water.

'You don't have to hold that tar-pole-eon so close around you,' Pursely said. 'Nobody's left in this world but you and me and the oxens, and all of us has seen a nekkid boy before.'

It was true. Cav gaped north, where the herd should have been, and then east and west and even south. But the Kane and Cavanagh outfit was gone, cows, cavvy, mule wagon and all.

'What happened?' Cav asked. After he asked it, he thought it was kind of a dumb thing to say.

'Cow-brutes run ahead of the storm, I reckon,' Pursely said. 'It's a thing they sometimes do. Be all right, if they don't hit a floody spot and drown their fool selves. Rest of the outfit took off after them, accidental or on purpose.

Probably the riders rode out of an attachment and a devotion to the cows; and the remuda run out of love for the drovers; and the mules run because everybody else did.'

'So what do we do?'

Pursely said: 'Hang our clothes on a hick'ry limb. I mean, we drape our shirts and pants and other possibles on the tailgate, an' let the good sun dry them out. And then we drive, wearin' our little pink skins and hoping no passing tintyper comes along to make a permanent picture of our predicament. You drive and I will get a box of wet sand on the tail of the wagon and pour enough coal oil on it to boil some water.'

But the chill was going; the hot Texas sun was getting back to its usual burn. Ahead of them the storm was a black cloud on the ground, and then it was gone, either rained out or over a hill and down too low to be seen.

The wagon canvas steamed, the oxen steamed, the ground steamed and Pursely steamed, going about his job in his long underwear.

Pursely brought him a cup of hot coffee, heavily sugared, and said: 'Get that down and you'll live. You're all over bruises, where the rain beat you into the side of the wagon, or someplace.'

Cav looked down. His arms and legs were considerably black and blue; he ached all over. The coffee did help, and when he put his clothes on again, they were still wet, and that felt good against the rising heat.

He kept looking ahead, but the prairie was too wet for the herd to throw up dust.

Wet ground and soft ground. The well-greased wheels of the wagon didn't creak, the oxen's hoofs didn't thud, and so the rider passed within a half mile of them and never saw them.

He was a man Cav had never seen before, riding north, half dozing in his saddle. From his looks, and the looks of his outfit, he had been lucky, and just ridden behind the storm.

The rain had killed the heat-quavers that usually twisted the desert air; Cav could see plainly the man's face—neither young nor old, neither fat nor thin—his clothes, neither rich nor poor, the rifle under his leg, and his horse.

Or, rather, his mare.

The man was riding Belle.

Pursely was, for the moment, on the wagon box, taking a ride. He might have opened his mouth and whooped, but Cav jumped up on the hub and stopped him, at the same time calling to the oxen to whoa.

'You gone outa your head, Cav?'

Cav said: 'I got it to do! When you find the herd, tell Big Cav I saw my mare again, and took out after her. I got it to do, Pursely.'

The cook blinked his small eyes. 'Whatever it is, I don't know about it, but I sure know a sure-enough got-it-to-do look.'

'That's my mare that was stolen from me, and I was put in jail for it and——'

'Now, back up, boy, and tell it a piece at a time.'

But Cav shook his head. 'When I see you again! For now, I want a canteen of water and maybe some cold biscuits or something. I got to go see what that fellow's up to, Pursely. I'm sorry about having to leave you with no one to fetch your wood and water, but I just have to.'

'Got to, you got to. Won't kill me to do my own choring, though it won't benefit me, either. But you better tell me what it's all about.'

'Haven't got time.'

'All right,' Pursely said. 'All right. Here's a water bottle canteen. Here's an old hat of mine to keep the sun from frying what brains you got. Your boots are all right, yeah. . . . Take this can of bacon grease and give 'em a good going over tonight, after the soaking you got. . . . Hey, come back here. You don't need that ox-goad where you're goin', and maybe so I do, having oxen to drive.'

And Cav was off across the prairie.

He struck east, where he had seen the man, and some north, and cut his trail in about ten minutes. Then he settled himself to follow that trail.

It wasn't hard; it didn't take an Apache. The ground was drying out, but it still took hoof prints, and here and there they were full of water.

The worst trouble was the heat, which was steamy instead of its usual dry. But Cav walked along, going fast but not too fast. He had heard someplace that a man could keep up with a horse, especially a grass-fed horse, since the man could travel three or four hours a day longer than a horse could.

Pursely had given him a big canvas bag of cold biscuits and corncake to take along. He chewed them as he walked, from time to time, and didn't worry about water; every spring and seep and hollow in a rock was full, and he had his canteen.

The first night he camped so close to the stranger that he could smell his wood fire. When the fire died down, and he was pretty sure the man was asleep, Cav belly-crawled to where the man's mare was picketed out to graze.

By star shine, his eyes were pretty sure this was Belle. By feel, his hands made more sure of it; and when she nickered, real soft, and blew down the back of his neck, all of Cav was certain that he had found his mare again.

But the rider was not Shawnee, and that was a strange

thing. It didn't seem that the peddler would sell the mare, when he had gone to so much trouble to get her.

Maybe he had had a deal with this stranger, to buy Belle for him? Maybe the stranger was an outlaw, who couldn't come into a town and buy his own saddle horse, and had promised Shawnee a big lot of money to do the buying for him?

That was it. This was Jesse James or Sam Bass or another of those men the riders sometimes talked about around the fire or sang about to the cattle.

Even as he said it, Cav knew it wouldn't hold water. He remembered Shawnee too well; no outlaw of standing and consequence would have the peddler for an agent.

That wasn't it.

Then—

There wasn't any real explanation. Shawnee had had both mares when he dared the Groliers into the horse race. Maybe he had dared once too often, and this man had won Belle in a race.

If that was so, Cav had little chance of getting her back, and might end up in jail again, trying. . . . He wished Big Cav was here, or even Yonder or Pursely. . . .

There was still money in his purse, which—now he thought of it—he had left in his bedroll. And though Big Cav and he had never spoken of it, he supposed he was going to get paid something by Kane and Cavanagh at the end of the north-drive. Maybe if he just picked himself up like a man and walked into the stranger's camp, the man would agree to bring Belle to Abilene, Kansas, and sell her to Cav. . . .

And maybe he had better play it sneaky and Comanche-like for a while.

Cav went back a couple of rises and cold-camped behind

114

a rock, lying in a patch of sand that was reasonably dry, and waiting for morning.

All the next day he trailed the stranger again. It was not at all bad travelling, not after bringing a bull-team and a wagon through that dry jornada; but there didn't seem to be much sense to it, hanging around the fringes of the stranger's notice, like a little kid hoping to be picked for a team in the big boys' ball game.

That second day there were dust clouds on the prairie. That one ahead, not too far, was the Kane and Cavanagh outfit, he was sure; back of them, maybe ten miles and maybe a little more, that would be the Groliers.

It made Cav feel better just to see the dust thrown up by his friends. He thought he'd be back with them soon.

But the stranger cut off to the west, finding a trail up through the rimrock off the driveway, and making Cav's job easier; in the rocky ridge country a man could travel a lot faster than a horse; sometimes Cav would be able to take a half-hour's good rest in the shade of a rock while the stranger led Belle through the shaky footing of frost-loosened rocks and tight-growing brush.

They came down on the valley floor again with the dust of K-C not more than three miles ahead. The stranger camped, and so did Cav, a couple of hundred yards behind him, fireless, but with a good canteen of water.

Night came, and the stranger didn't build a fire. He had Belle picketed in the middle of a natural wall, a cactus motte, they called it, a big tangle of prickly pear.

Cav watched, the stars wheeled, and night wore on. Cav must have fallen asleep, because he heard voices but he never heard Shawnee arrive at the stranger's camp.

Belly down, Cav wriggled up towards them. Moon was set, which was a blessing and a curse, because, while it kept

Cav unseen, it didn't do much to help him pick out rocks from cactus, grass from thorn. He got his hands pretty well prickled up, not to mention his belly and knees, through his clothes.

The men had built a tiny little fire, too small to be seen from the Kane and Cavanagh camp, but enough to show that the visitor was Shawnee, indeed. The men squatted by the fire and drank their coffee, and rolled cigarettes, and Cav watched. He was too far to hear, but plenty close for eye or gun; if he'd had even the oldest kind of a muzzle-loading pistol, he could have picked Shawnee off from right where he lay.

It was a good thing he had no kind of a gun, nor even a throwing knife.

He had to hear what they were saying! But as he wriggled in, something moved behind the men and their tiny fire, and for a minute he thought it was Belle; her well-shaped gentle head and nicely curved neck were plain against the stars.

Then the horse walked around its picket, and he saw it was Belle's sister, the stiff-legged mare.

The men both stood up, and the stranger took the mare's

halter. They started out in the night directly for Cav, and he got as low as he could in the sandy ground, finding some more sharp stones and a few thorns on the way.

He thought sure they were going to walk on him or pass close enough to see him, but all that happened was that old stiff-leg whickered a little as she passed; the men leading her paid her no heed.

He didn't dare follow them as they went into the cactus motte. He just waited, and pretty soon they came back out again, still leading.

Only this time they were walking faster; they had Belle on the end of the tie-rope.

He held his breath. He and stiff-leg had never been friends, but Belle was a different matter. She was liable to let out a real bellow, instead of a whicker, when she smelled him.

But just as she had raised her head, Shawnee jerked the halter-line and said: 'Come along, girl,' and she danced, so that any noise she made could be taken as coming from not liking the treatment she was getting, or at not wanting to leave her sister.

Back at the little campfire, the stranger made a step of his two hands, and Shawnee slipped up on Belle barebacked and rode off, using the halter for a hackamore.

Cav waited. Then the stranger could be seen, pulling off his boots and his hat, squinching back into his bedroll.

The fire flickered, and then went down to a glow, and then went all the way out.

The stranger never snored; it was mighty unaccommo- dating of him. But Cav gave him a good, long time to get to sleep, and then backtracked him to the cactus motte and into it, and to old stiff-leg.

She gave that little whicker again. Cav untied her, gently, gently, and doubled up the picket rope, coiled it around his arm. He led her out of the motte, and made a wide circle on the prairie, and finally slipped aboard old stiff-leg's back, and took off after Shawnee and Belle.

He rode the last mile leaning forward like a county-fair jockey, his hand clenched over the mare's nose to keep her from whickering. But it wasn't necessary; he came on Jerry and the night cavvy before he came on the Kane and Cavanagh camp.

Jerry was sitting his night-horse, right leg looped over the saddlehorn, just watching the horses, as they slept or lazily ate the good, wet prairie grass.

Cav rode right up to him, said: 'Had I a been a Louisiana 'gator, I could have bit your leg off.'

Jerry turned his head, said, slowly: 'Good thing you wasn't, then. Where you been, Cav? All Pursely saw to say was that you had some business of your own. I been rustling wood and water for him, till I'm tuckered.'

'Peddler camped with the boys?'

'Plumb crazy peddler,' Jerry said. 'He's got him an old rheumatic mare he plans to race against that little pony of Yonder's tomorrow dawn.'

'Peddler's mare in with the cavvy?'

'What *are* you up to, Cav?' Jerry shifted his head. 'That's the peddler-horse you are riding!'

Cav chuckled. 'One of them, Jerry. The other one's as fast as anything you ever saw, outside a lightning storm. Where's she picketed?'

'Halfway between here and—Cav, you sure you ain't been eating loco weed or falling on your head?'

'Show me, Jerry.'

Jerry looked over the horse herd that was his charge, satisfied himself that they were quiet, and nodded. Together, they rode towards camp. After a minute or so, Cav heard a noise he could never mistake; Belle's proud whicker.

At once he slid down from stiff-leg's back, and grabbed Jerry's reins. 'I'll hold both horses here. See can you sneak in and bring that mare out. I'd like to see Big Cav, too.'

Jerry said: 'Here's some parched corn. Drop a grain now and then, and I'll send the boss out to trail you.'

Jerry walked off, easy and soft and pigeon-toed in his boots.

Seemed to Cav that the wrangler was gone a day and a half. But the stars hadn't moved at all, to see, when Jerry was back, leading Belle. She and stiff-leg tried to nose each other, but each had a hand firmly clasped over her nose to make the meeting quiet.

Cav and Jerry switched ropes. It seemed to Cav that Jerry winked before he went back towards camp.

Distantly, a voice called: 'Who's out there?'

Jerry's Texas twang was soothing: 'Jes' the night wrangler, peddler. I'm seeing that your racing stable's fast tied.' He dropped his voice to a whisper. 'Boss is out looking over the bedding grounds, Cav. I'll send him after you when I see him.'

Night was a bad time to seek shelter in. A man and a horse might think themselves well hidden, and then have daytime show them up like a petticoat on a cow-camp washline.

Cav got down on his heels and studied the sky. Yonder, to the east, might be a low-lying cloud bank; but it might just as well be the first ridge of the foothills, too.

He led Belle out a good, safe distance, and then slipped up on her back. She rocked back and forth, gently, a few times, maybe to show she was glad he was on her back, and then his heel nudged her, and she went towards the black mass in a soft, easy lope.

Ground rose under her hoofs, and then rocks came alongside, and they were on a ridge. He found a good boulder and rode behind it, and slipped off. He tied Belle to a bush, strong enough to hold her, limber enough to keep her from breaking her tie rope.

He had pulled some dry grass and was rubbing Belle down when he heard a horse coming. He clamped his hand over Belle's nose to keep her quiet, but he didn't have to; Big Cav came riding around the rock, grinning.

The first thing he said was: 'Pretty mare you got there, mister. You planning on racing her?'

Cav said, gravely: 'I've heard tell that it isn't good for a road horse to race in company.'

Big Cav laughed out loud as he swung down and started working on Belle's off-side. They swiped slowly along her coat, getting the sweat off, working up a shine. 'Pursely thought you had lost your last wit, going off that way, Little Cav. Finally he happened to mention that you were following a man riding a pretty good-looking mare, and I figured out what you were up to. Two days later, when a peddler came in, pulled by a mule and a stiff-legged, pretty-headed mare, I knew he was planning to do us the way he did the Grolier boys.'

Cav said: 'But you let him into camp, anyway.'

Big Cav said: 'Why, I knew you were on his trail. I counted on you to catch up with him and fix things before the race.'

Little Cav felt his face getting red, felt a lump forming in his throat. When he could talk, he changed the subject: 'Who's racing him?'

'Yonder. We figure the fastest horse we have is his grulla.'

'Grulla?'

'Spanish for a mouse-coloured pony.'

Cav nodded. He knew the one.

Big Cav said: 'Get some sleep, and come in with first light. You'll want to see the race. Isn't it a nice night? Man could see to read a paper by that moon.'

'It won't keep me awake,' Cav said. 'I have trailed a long and weary way today.'

But when he lay down, he just had time to take his hat off before he was asleep.

Once he woke up, thinking someone was coming; but it was Belle, getting down on the ground to lie near him.

First flush of dawn woke him; he came out from behind the rock, and looked around. He could not see the Kane and Cavanagh camp, he could not even see the valley floor. He followed a downhill deer track, Belle crying out behind him at being left. He called back that she'd have breakfast soon. . . .

Ten minutes later he could see the valley, and the camp. He'd picked himself a first-class spot, with as good a view as a church steeple; but he wanted to hear, too.

So he went on down, picking cover when he could, darting across the open spaces when he had to.

There had been no need to hurry. He came out behind a little rise, and by pressing down into the ground, he could just see the ears and crown of Belle's sister. Raising himself cautiously, he saw Big Cav and Shawnee, pacing off a quarter mile runway; and behind them, Jerry bringing in the night cavvy, and the men stringing ropes from the bed-wagon tongue to hold them, and Pursely getting breakfast. Hiram was doing the wood-and-water chores, which was a wonder; Cav had never seen the bed-wagon driver do anything much but drive before.

Billy and Bo were staked near the chuck wagon, turning over ears of corn between their teeth. They looked just fine, which was no surprise, since it was only a few days since Cav had left them.

Now the cavvy was inside its rope corral, and Yonder was unfurling a throw-rope. It whistled through the air—Cav could hear the noise plain—and settled on the neck of the grulla, Yonder's mouse-coloured streak of lightning.

The grulla came out of the herd on his hind legs, striking a little with his front hoofs, but just playfully. Cav could hear Yonder saying: 'Now, Mouse, easy, Mouse.'

The peddler, Shawnee, was taking a tin cup of coffee from Pursely. Shawnee's old bridle hung over his left arm. He said: 'Now, there are fellas don't believe in eating nor drinking nothing before a race; makes extra weight, they say, and might give the rider a stitch in the side. But, way I figure it, after I take all you fellas' money, you might not feel favourable towards my drinking your coffee.'

Jerry, his work done for the day, sauntered up. 'You talk big, peddler. Got any more money?'

'Could be.'

Big Cav said: 'Jerry, you've drawn all I'm of a mind to advance you. The grulla is fast, but he might stumble.'

Jerry said: 'Now, boss, this is a poor wrangler's chance to buy a farm. . . . No? Then, peddler, what'll you bet against my saddle there?'

Shawnee dickered and he fussed, and he finally put up twenty-five dollars. The saddle was worth more.

It seemed to Cav that Jerry and Big Cav had spread the word around; the boys were pushing their bets at Shawnee now; saddles and bridles, belt-guns and even the silver bands some of them wore on their hats. Larry, who usually rode left swing, put up a pair of gold-mounted spurs that were his pride; he had never worn them on the drive, just gotten them out to brag on.

Cav began to feel funny in the stomach. But—there was the stiff-legged mare on her picket line, and there, behind him, was Belle. But was he sure? They certainly looked an awful lot alike.

Yonder rode up on the grulla, now, and looked down at Shawnee. 'I'm ready to go if you are,' he said. 'Yonder stands our chance to find out which horse is the faster; we'll never learn any younger.'

Shawnee nodded. He handed the tin cup to Pursely, and walked towards the picket pin. 'No saddle?' Yonder called after him.

When Shawnee didn't answer, Yonder slipped off the grulla, and uncinched. One of the hands helped him shuck the saddle off, and Yonder slipped back up on Mouse's back. A patch of dark on the mouse-coloured back was sweat, though the day was not yet hot. Showed the grulla was eager, and knew something was up, seemed like.

Shawnee fastened both ends of the curb-strap to one side, like he didn't want to take any chances of pulling by mistake and holding the mare up. Then he bellied up on the mare's back and slid a leg over.

When he picked up the reins, the mare walked out.

Cav's stomach went back where it belonged. That walk never belonged to Belle.

It was a good, long distance from Cav to Shawnee, but even so, Cav could see the lean face go grey above the whiskers, almost a fish-belly white. The mare went towards the starting point at her curious walk.

Shawnee swayed on the bare back, and grabbed at his belly. 'I'm sick,' he yelped. 'Musta been something in the coffee.'

Big Cav pushed over to the mare. She was walking away from him, but he had no trouble catching up to her. 'You

saying my cook poisoned you?'

Shawnee said: 'No, no. Just a little sick . . . you boys ride along, and I'll catch you tonight and we'll race in the morning.'

The boys were muttering like bees in a hollow tree. Cav stood up and started walking towards the camp. The time for hiding was over.

Yonder circled the grulla and rode back. 'Race was for today,' he said. 'You dee-faulting, peddler?'

Cav walked on in.

Shawnee was looking around the circle of riders. Some of them weren't wearing guns—Hiram never wore one, Pursely seldom, the men on drag usually saved themselves the heavy pull on their hips, since a man on drag was not likely to see anything to shoot at.

But there were several guns there. And a great many

heavy hands and well-muscled shoulders. Shawnee gulped, his whiskers fluttering. 'I'll ride,' he said.

Nobody helped him slide back onto stiff-leg's back, but he made it, put his leg over, picked up the reins that ran to the uncurbed bit.

There was something funny about that, Cav thought. Belle's sister didn't need a curb strap. She really didn't need a bit at all; she lived with one ear cocked for the welcome word: 'Whoa.'

Shawnee pulled the mare around, a little roughly, and this brought him facing Cav, strolling into camp, perhaps fifty feet away from Shawnee and the mare.

The peddler's chin came up till his whiskers stuck straight out. His hands pulled the reins way back; if the strap had been in place, old stiff-leg would have reared. Shawnee opened his mouth to say something.

But he never said it, because Big Cav came over and dropped a hand on Cav's shoulder. 'This is our chuck wagon driver and cookie, peddler,' he said. 'Too bad he's too late to bet on this race, but, then, I don't exactly approve of young 'uns betting. Do you?'

Shawnee shut his mouth again.

Yonder said: 'There's the running course, yonder, and here's my grulla getting cold under my legs. Let's go, peddler.'

Side by side, the grulla dancing, the mare walking as grave as a preacher leading a funeral, they rode out to the starting line scratched in the dust, a quarter mile away.

Several of the riders slipped on their ponies and rode out along the course.

Cav went to stand near Big Cav, who spoke up in a quiet voice, though Cav could hear the laugh under it. 'Young 'uns shouldn't bet,' he said. 'They shouldn't be taught bad habits, or treated bad, either. They are the future of Texas.'

His hand on Cav's shoulder shook a little, and Cav knew the big man was laughing inside. He had trouble keeping his own laughter down. He said: 'I don't feel like the future of Texas. I feel hungry.'

Big Cav let out a short whoop, and then pressed his lips together.

The horses stood at the starting point. A rider named Joe had his gun out, pointed at the sky. He fired, and they saw the puff of smoke and then heard the crack of the pistol, and the riders started for them and the finish line.

Well, that is, the grulla started. Old Mouse came tearing home, Yonder crouched up on his withers, flailing with his rein-ends, not looking back.

Stiff-leg came walking after him, step after patient step. She was a good ten feet from the starting line when Yonder was over the finish and dropping off his sweaty pony.

Yonder's feet were on the ground, he had handed his halter over to Jerry before he looked back, and saw that Shawnee had hardly covered half of the quarter mile. His mouth flew open. He said: 'Yonder is the most humorous thing I ever saw, yonder.'

Big Cav suddenly let out a wild guffaw.

Shawnee rode up to them, and slid down, and stood, stiff and thin and like he knew he didn't have a prayer. Big Cav said: 'Get out your betting tickets, boys. The peddler pays.'

Shawnee began sweating, all across his forehead, the water running down his thin cheeks in streams, and into his whiskers. A minute later, the whiskers started to drip.

Big Cav said: 'Hiram first, then Jerry, then Pursely, then Yonder and the rest of the boys. I come last, peddler.'

Hiram said: 'I bet you my shotgun and twenty dollars agin' yo're buggy and mule.'

'Take it,' Shawnee said.

Jerry said. 'Thirty dollars and my six-gun against forty dollars and your peddler's pack.'

Shawnee said: 'Take it.'

Hiram: 'I still got my twenty dollars, Jerry. Sell me the pack? I am plain full up to here with driving bed wagon. I aim to start life as a peddler and become rich and——'

Jerry was the only one listening to him. From Pursely on through the riders, all the bets had been cash. Back in Alex, Shawnee had not had enough money to buy Belle; but since then he had played his crooked horse-racing rig on the Groliers and maybe on other outfits. He was rich.

Had been rich. Now the money rolled out, slowly at first, and then faster, as his hands peeled off the bills, working deftly, as though he wanted to get rid of the money and be done with it.

There was not quite enough money to pay off Big Cav, the last of the betters.

Big Cav said: 'There is a grey horse back with the Grolier outfit that belongs to you. This boy here took him for a little ride. You mind, peddler?'

Shawnee shook his head.

'You can wait here for him,' Big Cav said. 'The Groliers'll be trailing through here in three, four days. I'll write you a note to them.'

Shawnee shook his head. In a strange, croaking voice, like a dying crow, he said: 'I owe you money, Mister—Mister——'

'Cavanagh. They call me Big Cav.'

Shawnee looked from Cav to Big Cav. 'Kinfolk?'

'Could be,' Big Cav said, and stood.

Shawnee said: 'I owe you money, Mr. Cavanagh. Owe you money.' He seemed to have aged; Cav didn't think he had ever seen an older man. 'Let me work for you, pay it back.'

Yonder said, curiously: 'What you scared of, peddler? There's no ghosts yonder.'

'Partner,' Shawnee said. 'Got a partner.'

'I saw him,' Cav said. 'He swapped Belle for that mare. I——'

Big Cav dropped a hand on his shoulder, shushing him. 'You think your partner may gun for you?'

Shawnee croaked: 'I know it.'

Pursely said, softly: 'Hiram's quitting, Big Cav.'

Big Cav said: 'Yea, yeah. . . . Jerry, you've been saying you couldn't sleep well, days, in the bed wagon. . . . You take over Hiram's mule team.'

Jerry said: 'Yes, sir.'

Big Cav said: 'Peddler—Shawnee—you're cookie. Pursely here's your boss. You goad his oxen, and you fetch his wood and water, and you do what he says, or you don't eat.'

Shawnee said: 'Thank you, sir, thank you.' He was a long way down from the man who had talked so slick to the sheriff, who had stolen Belle, put Cav in jail and——

'Leaves you, Cav,' Big Cav said. 'Leaves you out of a job. Small thanks after the turn you did us, making us all rich men. But you're night wrangler. You'll be a cowboy yet, Cav. . . . There's a mare up on that ridge I want you to throw into the cavvy, and then you'd better crawl into the bed wagon and get some sleep; you've got a night wrangle ahead of you.'

Cav said: 'Yes, sir.'

Pursely, still holding his roll of money said: 'Not afore he eats, boss. No sleepin' on an empty belly for that night wrangler.'

Big Cav threw back his head and whooped. Then he said: 'Outfit's turning into a bunch of nursemaids! Head 'em north, boys, and keep 'em travellin'! We got a lot of cows and a lot of miles to Kansas.'

Glossary of words used in the South-Western United States

BLACKSTRAP   a very heavy treacle, so called because of its appearance when poured. This word is common in all parts of the United States.

BRONC SHOES   lightweight horseshoes, made of iron soft enough to be shaped in the field without the use of a forge. They are sometimes called 'cold' shoes. 'Bronc' is from the Spanish 'bronco', meaning 'wild'.

CHAPS   short for 'chaparejos' (Spanish), heavy leather coverings for the legs, necessary when riding the chaparral, or thorny brush thickets of the South-West and Mexico.

CINCHED DOWN   tightened, fastened, from the Spanish 'cincha', a girth.

CRAWDADS   crayfish, in the Middle or Far West.

DUDE   a fancy fellow, or any Easterner. Origin unknown, though possibly from 'duds', clothing.

HUISACHE BUSH   a sub-family, rather than a species of low trees or tall shrubs related to the acacias and mimosas, thorny, with elaborate flowers, and producing an edible pod.

LULU   a somewhat old-fashioned American slang word for anything superlatively good, bizarre, or outrageous.

PONES   cakes of cornmeal and water (the corn being maize, of course). The name comes from a Southern corruption of 'poor', since no simpler or cheaper food can be found.

SOWBELLY   is simply salt pork.

TINTYPER   photographer, especially an itinerant one. At the time of our story men wandered around the United States and other countries, taking portraits with wet cameras that printed on tin. The process was very fast, but the pictures were inclined to fade in a few months.